THE
DEER-JACKERS

THE DEER-JACKERS

By *ALF EVERS*

Illustrated by Lewis Parker

THE OVERLOOK PRESS

WOODSTOCK · NEW YORK

First published in 1997 by
The Overlook Press, Peter Mayer Publishers, Inc.
Lewis Hollow Road
Woodstock, New York 12498

Library of Congress Cataloging-in-Publication Data

Evers, Alf.
  The deer-jackers / Alf Evers.
  p.   cm.

  Summary: Denny convinces his Uncle Frank and cousin Bert to help
him uncover the sinister ploy of some deer poachers near his family's property.
[1. Deer—Fiction. 2. hunting—Fiction. 3. Poaching—Fiction. 4. Mystery and
detective stories.]   I. Title
PZ7.E9227De   1996   [Fic]—dc20   96-3580

ISBN 0-87951-649-6
Manufactured in the United States of America

9 8 7 6 5 4 3 2 1

Contents

Contents

THE
DEER-JACKERS

1) Mystery in the Hollow

DENNY OPENED his eyes halfway and then closed them again. He wriggled on his bed in the dark attic bedroom.

Arh-Arh-Arh-Arh!

Denny's eyes opened wide. No, he wasn't dreaming. That was Boot he heard. The dog was standing in front of the woodshed in the light of the September moon barking at a mysterious something moving in the night. Maybe a solemn porcupine was waddling by on his way to a dessert of apples in the old orchard that almost surrounded the Meech house. Maybe a raccoon was heading for the garbage can beside the kitchen door, hoping that the cover wouldn't be fastened down this time. Or maybe a faint whiff of bear or wildcat had drifted down to Boot's sensitive nose from high up on the side of the dark mountain that hung over Meech Hollow.

Denny straightened his pillow and settled down to go to sleep again. He would have to be up on time the next morning because he had an arithmetic test to face in school. This was no time to be wishing he could be outside in the moonlight. Then suddenly Denny sat bolt upright. He stared at the two windows of his room. What was that he had just seen? What had made him wake up so quickly? A few seconds passed before Denny got the answer. It hadn't been any change in Boot's barking—that was still echoing steadily against the mountain wall. No, something had moved across his windows. A glow had lighted up the small windowpanes and passed like a stealthy ghost across the slanting ceiling.

But where could the light have come from? It could not have come from the headlights of a car. There was no road on that side of the house; and besides, no sound but Boot's barking had broken the normal music of a September night. Maybe someone had turned a flashlight toward the house.

Denny jumped out of bed. Whatever was going on, one thing was sure: he would have to investigate. And investigating mysterious happenings was what he'd been dreaming about lately. Once he'd wanted to be an airplane pilot when he grew up and he made model planes and zoomed and dived as he walked. Another time he'd wanted to be an auto mechanic, and that time he tinkered with Mom's toaster until it burned the toast and shot it six feet in the air. But at last he really knew what he wanted to do. He'd be a scientist who investigated mysterious things and made great discoveries, the way they said Isaac Newton did when he discovered the law of gravitation by watching an apple falling from a tree.

You couldn't tell what that light across his windows might mean. Lately some people had been saying they'd seen strange things in the mountains at night. Some said there were devils on the loose in the Catskills. Well . . . maybe they were seeing weird beings from another planet. Maybe some of these had turned a luminous ray unlike anything known on earth against the Meech house. You couldn't let a chance to be in on a thing like that go by even if you had a hundred arithmetic tests to take the next day.

Denny tiptoed down the narrow stairs. He moved carefully because he didn't want to wake up the rest of the family, Mom and Dad and his little brother Hank. He skipped the second stair from the bottom because it creaked. Then he made his way across the living room by a combination of keeping his hands stretched out ahead of him and trying to remember exactly where everything was.

Crash! Denny stopped and stood still. His legs had hit the rockers of Mom's chair. She must have moved it a few feet toward the kitchen door the night before. The crash didn't awaken anybody—it was as silent in the house as a church on Monday morning. Denny unfroze. He slowly opened the front door and slipped outside.

Denny came to the woodshed. His bare feet made no sound at all on the cool dewy grass. Boot went right on barking. "What is it, Boot?" Denny whispered. Boot wagged his tail in greeting and kept right on barking.

But the way Boot barked told Denny something. The dog wasn't giving the quick, excited bark he saved for strangers coming up the road or for cats sneaking up from the valley to find out what the mice of Meech Hollow tasted like. No, this was the kind of bark that meant that whatever was bothering Boot was too far away to be much of a threat to the Meech family. Maybe it was only another dog following a fox's trail through the brush lot on the far side of the orchard. Maybe a hungry skunk was turning over stones at the edge of the hemlock woods in search of a few crickets for dinner.

"What's it all about, Boot?" Denny asked.

The dog's barking ended in a happy little snort. He sniffed at the long stretch of bare leg showing below Denny's blue pajamas—Denny was growing so fast that everything he had was getting too small for him. Boot wagged his tail cheerfully. Then he stared down the long rows of apple trees and barked again—*Arh-Arh-Arh-Arh!* There *was* something worth barking at among the dim trees across the lane. But what could it be?

Denny wished then that he had the kind of nose his dog had. A nose that could tell him who was out there under the faint moon and twinkling stars. A nose like that would be a big help to a scientist. Denny strained his nose to its utmost. But all he got was a rich damp smell of leaves and earth. He heard the brisk chirping of the insects making the most of the few days they had left before the frost would end their chirping forever.

From way up the mountain came the humming of the wind among the oak and pine trees. Boot pushed his wet nose against Denny's leg. Denny petted the dog. Boot stiffened and pulled away. *Arh-Arh-Arh-Arh!* he barked toward the orchard. Denny thought he heard a muffled sound from among the dark trees—or did he imagine it?

At that moment the wind, which had been working its way down the mountain, struck. A cool current of air flowed around Denny and set the woodbine knocking at the woodshed. Boot stopped barking. He yawned and stretched. The wind had cut off the sound and scent that had aroused him. He lay down as if getting set for a nap. As far as Boot was concerned the fun was over.

"O.K., Boot. That's it," Denny whispered. He crouched and rubbed the old dog's head as he stared for a moment into the quiet orchard. Then he tiptoed up-stairs and wriggled into bed. It felt hot and stuffy after the coolness outside. It was a long time before Denny felt sleep whirling him away.

Then—there it was again. Denny was awake. He was sitting up in bed and down below Boot was barking, *Arh . . . Arh . . . Arh . . .* The dog hammered away at it slowly as if he expected to keep it up for the rest of the night and didn't want to wear himself out too soon. Again there was a light at the window but a faint one this time. Boot's bark speeded up and took on an urgent sound as if a stranger was moving close to him.

Just then the old clock downstairs struck loudly—

one, *two*, *three*, *four*. As Denny listened to the last stroke he felt his body relaxing. Even with Boot's clamor in his ears his head found the pillow and he fell asleep.

He didn't wake up until Mom called him to breakfast for the third time. He dressed fast but by the time he got to the kitchen Dad was gone and was halfway to the Spacemaster plant in the valley. He worked there making parts for some kind of space vehicle. He'd been doing that ever since he'd given up trying to make a living raising apples in the Hollow, and Denny didn't see him at breakfast unless he got up right on the dot. It was too bad this morning because Denny wanted to ask Dad whether he'd heard anything during the night. Mom wasn't much help—she had slept right through the night. Hank wasn't any help either—he was only five. He said he was sure he'd heard something. It was a couple of bears growling at each other. That was Hank, all right; he never wanted to be left out of anything.

"I hope it isn't the folks from back of the mountain," said Mom. She opened Denny's egg for him. "I just hope they're not up to something again." Mom shook her head.

"I hope not," Denny said gloomily. You never knew about the folks back of the mountain, he thought. Once Dad said their trouble was not being willing to admit that the twentieth century had come and was half gone. They were still living on their farms in narrow Yankee

Hollow much the way their grandfathers had done. Growing buckwheat and making maple syrup. Hunting and trapping and catching big trout in little brooks nobody else could get a minnow in. Every once in a while they would start a ruckus. Like the time Uncle Frank Meech refused to pay his school tax because the new central school was going to be called the Mountain Valley School. A place could be either a mountain or a valley but it couldn't be both at the same time, Uncle Frank said. And he'd won out that time. That was why the school Denny might miss getting to on time that morning was simply called Mountain Central.

Plenty of times the back-of-the-mountain cousins didn't make out that well. Maybe they'd have the wrong kind of license for one of the beat-up jeeps they drove. Maybe one of them would trap a mink out of season because he didn't keep up with the way the law changed. They didn't have radios, let alone television, back of the mountain, and they didn't read the papers—Cousin Tim Bridger said there wasn't any news worth reading these days. Yet they were good people. Every Sunday they dressed up and went down to the church at Turner's Crossroads and they sang hymns twice as loud as anybody else. They were always ready to drop everything and help anybody who was in trouble. Maybe they were out of step with the rest of the world, but Denny liked them. Half the time he wanted to lead the kind of life they did. The other half he played around with becoming a space agent and tracking down violators of space laws trying to rustle giant cattle on Mars.

"It sounds like something the back-of-the-mountain folks might have a hand in," Mom said. "They've been awfully quiet lately and it's about time they were heard from. Since that time Art Turner got the whole Simmons family stung when he took the wild honey from that hollow basswood tree there hasn't been a peep from them. You tell Dad what you heard and saw last night, Denny. Don't forget. Now come on—let's hurry." Mom got up fast.

There were some questions Denny wanted to ask Mom. But there wasn't any time. Mom had to drive Denny to the bus—if they weren't too late already. She had to drop Hank off at Mary Alstop's nursery school and then get to the Standley Laboratories, where she did typing mornings. It turned out that Hank was wearing one shoe and one sneaker and that held things up. Finally Denny found the missing sneaker on top of the big closet in the kitchen, and they all rushed for the car.

Of course they missed the school bus and had to chase it for two miles before they caught up. Some people might think life in Meech Hollow was dull, Denny thought as he settled down in the back of the bus, but he knew it was mighty lively. That afternoon, for instance, he wouldn't sit down and watch TV when he got home. Instead he'd be prowling around looking for clues. He might find a shining piece of metal of a kind unknown on this earth. Then again it might be a footprint of one of those heavy boots the back-of-the-mountain people sent away to a place in Michigan for.

It was a bad day for clues. The crisp September weather of the past few days had turned damp and soggy. While Denny was working at his spaghetti and milk in the school cafeteria a big bump of thunder made the whole building shiver, and the rain came down like mad. It would take a pretty tough clue to survive a downpour like that if the rain was as heavy in Meech Hollow.

It had been even heavier in the Hollow. Denny knew that the minute he got off the bus and saw the litter of twigs and small stones the rushing water had scattered across the road. But right across the debris of the storm he saw something that made him pay attention. It was the track of a jeep made since the rain had stopped. Anybody could tell these were jeep tracks because they were closer together than the tracks of a car or truck and one of them showed the pattern of a standard jeep tire. And there was only one set of tracks. That meant whoever had gone up the road was still there. Had one of the back-of-the-mountain folks gone up the road? Well, that was possible.

Halfway up the steep and winding road the tracks did something they weren't supposed to do. Instead of going on up they made a sharp turn and vanished among the bushes along the road. They were following an old road that once led to a log cabin where an old deaf-and-dumb man named Elliott used to live way back in Grandpa's time. Now there was nothing left but a hole where the cellar had been and some tired-out lilac bushes. All around it the maple and birch trees were crowding in. A few years before, somebody had used that road when they hauled out some oak logs. It was still O.K. for a jeep even though it looked all grown over.

Denny pushed his way through the bushes as cautiously as he could. Queer things had been going on in the Hollow the night before. It would pay to be careful. But the bushes wouldn't cooperate. Soaked as they were, they rustled loudly, at the same time soaking Denny's shirt and dungarees. A branch underfoot managed to snap loudly in spite of being wet. Denny stopped and stared at a blaze of bright red up ahead. It wasn't a swamp maple getting a start on the rest of the trees in the Hollow by turning red a little before it was supposed to. No—it was something Denny had seen plenty of times before. It was his Uncle Frank's old jeep.

In a second or two Denny was facing all two hundred twenty pounds of Uncle Frank perched on the crumbling wall around old Elliott's cellar hole. Uncle Frank's corncob pipe was carefully parked beside him. He was hard at work munching at a little apple that looked as if it might be all the home a couple of dozen worms ever had.

"Hi, Denny!" Uncle Frank sang out in a voice some-what muffled by apple. "Have one of these here. Catch!" He tossed Denny a lopsided dark red apple. "That's what we used to call a Black Baldwin. A little early to be picking them, but they're all right! Only half a dozen on this tree you're standing under. I've got 'em all." Uncle Frank patted a bulging pocket.

Denny examined the apple and chose a likely place to bite. It didn't taste bad—not if you liked a hard sour apple that wasn't quite ripe.

Uncle Frank's deep voice rumbled on. "Used to be a nice orchard here. They say old Elliott sure knew how to grow fruit even if he couldn't say a word."

Denny nodded. He was busy trying to dodge traces of the worms which had been working on the apple ahead of him. At the same time he was trying to figure out what Mom called "a nice tactful way" of finding out whether Uncle Frank had been fooling around the or-chard the night before. Denny had never been much good at doing things tactfully. While he was worrying about it a worm startled him by staring from the apple and waving its head in a friendly way. That jolted a straight question out of Denny.

"Were you in the Hollow last night, Uncle Frank?" he asked. Uncle Frank gave him a long look from those faded-looking blue eyes of his. He rubbed his chin thoughtfully.

"Naw," he said at last, "I sleep good nights instead of

running around like some—except when I go coon
hunting. And I wasn't hunting any coons last night.
No sir!"

That seemed to settle that. But there was another
question buzzing around in Denny's head like a bumble-
bee lost in an attic. What was Uncle Frank doing sitting
by an old cellar hole eating wormy apples? Denny didn't
try to be tactful. "You're not hunting coons now, are
you?" he asked.

"I'm not," said Uncle Frank. He worked one of his
big hands into a pocket of his blue denim jacket and
brought out a crumpled piece of paper. "I'm what you
might call apple hunting," he said. "Take a look at that
piece of paper and you'll see why. Wouldn't show that
to just anybody. But seeing you're one of the family, I'll
let you in on it."

Right away Denny knew where the scrap of printed
paper had come from. It was part of a page from *The
Rural Messenger and Hearthside Companion*. That was
a very old-fashioned sort of magazine the back-of-the-
mountain people took. They ranked it practically next
to the Bible. It didn't have any news in it. Just stuff
about how to can things, mend plows, and grow beans.
The ad on the page made Denny blink:

ONE THOUSAND DOLLARS
The above sum will be paid for an apple tree of the
variety known as the Golden Esopus. This variety is

known to have been grown in the Catskill Mountains region before 1900 but is no longer in cultivation. Address Messenger Box 334.

"If I remember right," said Uncle Frank, "there was an apple old Elliott and Grandpa Meech used to grow that some people called the Golden Esopus. We called ours the Fence apple because it grew by a fence. It could be there's still a tree around somewhere and that's what I'm looking for. I don't pretend to know why any man would offer a thousand dollars for one. But if anybody's fool enough to pay that money, I've got the sense to take it—if I can."

Denny was interested right away. "What's a Golden Esopus apple like?" he asked.

"If it's what I think it is—and, mind, I'm not sure—it's nothing special to look at. Just a little yellow apple with a kind of deep dimple where the stem grows. I remember eating some when I was a boy. Not much of an apple to my way of thinking. Give me a good Baldwin any day. But Grandma Meech thought a lot of them. A great one for apples, she was."

"What about those old trees in back of our orchard?" Denny asked. "They're the oldest ones around, I guess. If you go along this road it'll take you right to them."

"Naw," said Uncle Frank. He didn't say why.

"I'll take a look," Denny said. "I might as well go on home that way."

Uncle Frank objected that Denny would get all wet. He went to his jeep and opened the door. "Come on, get in. I'll run you home," he said. Denny shrugged his shoulders and climbed aboard, and Uncle Frank backed the jeep to the Hollow Road. As Denny got out at his house Uncle Frank stared at him and smiled. "Good luck finding that tree," he said heartily. And then he added in a lower voice, "Say, if you happen to see or hear anything queer going on in the Hollow by night— why, let me know, will you? Won't do to go butting into things by yourself. Might be dangerous." Without waiting for an answer Uncle Frank swung the jeep around and headed down the lane.

Denny watched the jeep until it disappeared behind the big maple trees at the turn in the road. His uncle had headed him off from going up the old road toward the back of the orchard. Why? Now he had given him a warning against investigating what was going on in the Hollow by night. Again, why?

From the kitchen came the sound of Mom and Hank laughing. They'd stop for a minute and then the laughter would break out again louder than ever. Denny wanted to find out what was so funny. He could smell a batch of Mom's ginger cookies just out of the oven. But if he went inside Mom would be sure to notice how wet his clothing and his sneakers were. She'd make him change and then when he went across the orchard he'd get wet again—and then Mom would be mad.

Denny slung his books down on the porch and made for the orchard. He cleared the stone wall in a jump and slowly walked across the grass. The place had been mowed a few weeks before and it was almost as smooth as a lawn with the old trees dotting it. Here and there was a gap where a tree had broken down and been cut up for firewood. Yellow jackets were working at the fallen apples which lay under every tree. A crow cawed in warning and half a dozen other crows cawed in reply as they flapped upward from the far end of the orchard. A chipmunk, who had been pulling an apple apart for the sake of its seeds, whistled at Denny and raced for the safety of the stone wall. He sat on the wall and scolded noisily. So far everything seemed normal for a September afternoon in Meech Hollow. Plenty of clues, but they were all to the doings of animals and insects.

Almost at the line where the orchard ended and the unmowed brush lot began, Denny's eyes picked up a faint track that hadn't been made by an animal. It had been pressed into the sod by the wheels of a jeep turning and then plunging back into the brush lot from which it had come. It would have come and gone by the road past the old Elliott place—that was sure. Had Uncle Frank driven here that very afternoon? Denny examined the tracks carefully and he didn't feel sure. They didn't look that fresh. They could have been made the night before.

Then something white caught Denny's eye. It was an

apple core, and the core hadn't turned brown. That looked like part of a trail left by Uncle Frank. But then the cores of some apples turned brown fast, others more slowly. Denny shook his head. The clues he was finding were getting him more confused than anything else.

There was one way to straighten things out—that was by following those jeep tracks. Denny headed toward the brush lot. It was funny, he was thinking as he pushed aside the dripping branches, but wasn't there a wire fence somewhere across this old road? Whoever drove this way would have to take the time to pull the fence down. Doing that would be sure to leave even more clues—footprints and toolmarks, for instance, and maybe things that popped out of a pocket when somebody leaned over.

It wasn't too easy to follow the trail because the dense bushes closed after anything went by, like the waves on the sea after a ship. But in a little while the trail led into a patch of woods where the bushes stopped and the jeep tracks could be plainly seen as they moved like two snakes down a rocky slope. Here and there the rain of that afternoon had trickled down the old road and washed out the tracks.

Denny rounded a curve and came to a quick stop. Right ahead was the wire fence stretching across the road. And there were the jeep tracks going up to it and right through it, for they continued on the other side. Suddenly Denny felt a little frightened. There was something almost spooky about it. People on this planet didn't go right through wire fences with jeeps without leaving them battered down. What was that Uncle Frank had said? 'Might be dangerous butting in all by yourself'—something like that. Well, here he was butting in all by himself. He looked around to see if Boot was there. Where was Boot anyway?

The old dog hadn't been around that morning. He hadn't come out as usual, jumping and wagging his tail when Denny came home that afternoon. Denny stared at the fence as if it might be possible to stare that confusing piece of evidence out of existence. He felt very small and very young and a little like giving up trying to find out what was going on in the Hollow.

At that moment something heavy began pressing against Denny's shoulder. He glanced down and saw a large brown human hand. From behind came a soft human voice asking, "What are you looking for here, young man?"

Denny thought he would never get the nerve to turn around and face whoever was behind him. At least it wouldn't be a strange being from out in space—the hand and the voice were perfectly human. That thought slowed down the shivers that had been chasing each other up and down Denny's spine. He turned and faced the man behind him.

2) The Deer-Jackers at Work

AT FIRST Denny was aware of nothing but two brown eyes fixed upon him. Everything else, the trees and bits of cloudy sky, and the man's face and clothing seemed to be nothing but a blur surrounding those two eyes. Then Denny woke up and recognized the tall man in the gray hat and green jacket. He was Jesse Ames, the game protector who turned up in the Hollow every now and then.

Ames smiled. "Oh, you must be the Meech boy— Denny. Didn't spot you from the back. You've grown a lot since I saw you last."

Denny felt a little ashamed of himself. Ames had come close enough to put a hand on his shoulder and he hadn't known he was there! Not so good for a boy who had been running around the woods ever since he was old enough to run at all and who was dreaming of being an investigator of mysterious happenings when he grew up. Denny smiled but his smile didn't have much power behind it.

"I was taking a look—" he began in answer to the

question Ames had asked when he put that hand on his shoulder. He had started the sentence but there didn't seem to be any way of finishing it. "I was taking a look," he repeated.

"Sure," Ames agreed pleasantly, "but a look at what?"

There wasn't anything to do with those eyes on him in that friendly but firm way but to tell his story. Denny talked about the light he'd seen the night before, about Boot's barking, about how he'd gone out and seen nothing unusual.

"Um-hum," said Ames. He waited for Denny to say more. Out it came about those jeep tracks he'd been following. But Denny didn't say anything about Uncle Frank or the apple core. He told himself he kept quiet about that because it wasn't important. But all the while he knew that he was obeying an old code of the mountain people that calls for sticking by your own folks—and Uncle Frank was Dad's cousin.

Jesse Ames stared through the woods in the direction of the Meech house. "Um-hum," he murmured again. He seemed to be thinking hard. Was he trying to see what the facts he already knew meant when added to those Denny had given him?

Denny did some putting things together himself, adding to what he'd seen and heard the fact of Jesse Ames's presence in the Hollow.

"Are you looking for deer-jackers?" he blurted out.

Ames wasn't very helpful. "There's been a lot of talk about them lately," he said, still staring up the Hollow.

Ames was putting it mildly, Denny thought. There had been those four men down in Orange County arrested for shooting deer by night and turning them into hamburger. They had turned a bright light on the deer in somebody's orchard where the deer were eating fallen apples. The deer had stared at the light as if fascinated —all deer seem to act that way when they see a bright light. Then the men had sneaked up close and shot the deer. That kind of hunting was called jacking and it was illegal. And that wasn't all. Somebody in Tarrentville had found five dressed deer hanging in his garage when he came back to his summer place unexpectedly. Plenty of people had reported hearing shots at night in places where nobody had any business being.

"This is the kind of place that would draw deer-jackers all right. That old orchard of yours is sure-fire deer bait, especially in a year like this when there isn't much for a deer to eat higher up the mountain. Usually they don't come down to eat the fallen apples this early."

Denny nodded. Every winter he'd seen deer working away in the orchard, even digging through the snow to get apples. Sometimes there were a dozen of them at a time on a moonlit night. And sometimes they'd go to the orchard even at noon if they were hungry enough.

"If all your people were out it isn't likely anybody

else would hear a shot fired up here," Ames went on. "You're in a kind of bowl with mountains all around. And at night somebody could keep an eye on you and jack deer after your lights were out and you were all asleep. Plenty of people will sleep through the sound of a couple of shots a few hundred yards away. I've known that to happen often."

Denny swallowed and shifted his feet a little. Could it be that some of those big-city toughs who people said were taking up deer-jacking were lurking in the Hollow —watching the comings and goings of the Meech family, sitting quietly in the brush around the orchard waiting for the lights in the house to go out? Meech Hollow had always seemed a very safe and snug place. It had seemed far away from all the evils of the world. But it didn't seem safe now.

Ames gave Denny a pat on the shoulder. "So long," he said. "Let me know if you see or hear anything unusual going on around here, will you? Ask your dad to let me know too." He scribbled a phone number on a card and handed it to Denny.

"O.K.," Denny said. He stuffed the card in his damp pocket and watched the game protector duck under the fence and vanish in the heavy laurel undergrowth. In a few minutes Ames would come to the place where Denny and Uncle Frank had met. What would he make of the signs he found there—the footprints and jeep tracks and those apple cores?

A wave of discouragement swept over Denny as he started homeward. The back-of-the-mountain folks might be in for a bad time. Years ago they had taken it hard when game laws began to be enforced. A lot of their food and income had come from hunting and trapping. For a while some of them had ignored the game laws, and people still remembered that. Not long ago some of the boys in school had teased Denny by singing a song somebody had made up years before about Denny's great-grandfather:

> *Old Billy Meech he had a gun,*
> *He shot a deer and then he run.*
> *They took him to the Kingston jail*
> *And now his gun is up for sale.*

Denny clenched his fists as he thought of how he had sailed into Ed Logan when he sang that dumb song after being warned. The new people who were building rows of neat houses in the valley never heard of the good things Billy Meech had done. Like planting those big maple trees along the Olderberg Road and cutting all the lumber to build the first two-room schoolhouse in town. Every time some of these people heard a bang in the woods out of hunting season they'd nod and say, "There go those Meeches again."

As Denny came near his house he unclenched his fists and gave a loud whistle for Boot. But the dog didn't race toward him. Boot was getting old now, but he was still ready to climb the mountains with Denny at a moment's notice. He was a little deaf, but that whistle had always brought him running—until this time. Denny was reaching for the knob of the kitchen door when he saw Boot coming out of the woodshed. The dog was wagging his tail in greeting. He stretched and then rolled on his back so that Denny could rub his chest.

"Boot acts tired," Mom called out from inside. "He doesn't want anything to eat. All he does is sleep."

"What's the matter, Boot?" Denny asked as he rubbed the dog's black fur. Boot rolled his eyes a little as if Denny had been scolding him.

"He's getting fat—that's what," said Denny.

Mom came out and looked at Boot. "He's fat as butter," she said. "We'll have to cut down on his dog food. Come inside, Denny, and see what I've got for you."

"Ginger cookies," Denny said, "you can smell them all over the Hollow."

Mom acted disappointed. "And I thought I was going to surprise you." She pretended she was going to cry. Then she laughed. "It isn't ginger cookies at all, it's gingerbread this time."

"Wow, that's even better," Denny exclaimed. And he dashed into the kitchen.

Maybe he ate too much gingerbread that afternoon. Maybe he had too much to think about. But Denny had a hard time getting to sleep that night. He hadn't told

Dad about what he'd heard and seen the night before. Dad was working late because of some mix-up at the plant. Denny went to bed with strange lights and sounds, Jesse Ames's face, and Uncle Frank's apple cores chasing each other around inside his head.

"ER 9-2827," Denny muttered. That was the telephone number Ames had given him. If anybody started anything that night he'd call the game protector right away. No, first he'd make sure it wasn't any of the back-of-the-mountain folks looking for apples or something like that. Wouldn't do to get them in trouble.

A muffled whirr, mingled with the insect sounds that filled the Hollow, invaded Denny's room. A plane crossing the mountain? Probably that was it. The whirr grew louder. No, that wasn't made by a plane. Dad's jeep was climbing up the Hollow Road. Yes, that was Dad shifting into second as he came to the steep place at the big rock. Denny listened as the jeep groaned up the lane and stopped. He heard the kitchen door opening and closing; he heard the voices of Mom and Dad. Pretty soon a hissing sound mixed with the voices. A delicious smell floated into the room. Mom was frying bacon! Dad was going to have a bacon and lettuce sandwich. Gosh, it smelled good. Hunger overpowered Denny. He'd risk a scolding and go right downstairs and ask Mom to make him a sandwich too. Then he could tell Dad all about the strange goings-on of the night before and that afternoon.

Once he'd made that decision, Denny felt quiet and peaceful. He made a move to get up and sank down in bed—asleep.

When Denny woke up it felt like the night before all over again. But this time it wasn't a light that was entering the room; it was a sound. The sound died away—and there it was again. A deep-voiced *Woo-ooo-ooo-ah! Aah! Aah! Aah!*

No doubt what that was! Denny sat up in bed. A pack of dogs was high above on the mountain. They were hot on the trail of something—probably a deer. They were flying along through the snarls of laurel and scrub oak all by themselves without any human companions. They were going wild for the moment and throwing off all they'd learned from hanging around with humans for thousands of years.

It was a bad thing when dogs formed packs and ran deer. If they were caught they could be shot—that was what the law said. Plenty of perfectly fine dogs somehow got in bad company and ran deer. It was up to the owner of a dog to see that he stayed close to home unless someone in the family took him into the woods.

But where was Boot? Usually when dogs were baying up in the mountain Boot sat by the woodshed and gave a short bark now and then as if he were saying, "Watch out, up there! Shame on you for going wild like that!" At least that was what Boot sounded like to

Denny. But tonight there wasn't a sound from Boot. There was only the faraway baying of the excited pack and nearby the chorus of the insects, with a katydid doing a solo.

In a few minutes Denny got up and slipped outside. He could never get to sleep until he made sure that Boot was all right. Maybe the dog was sick.

Boot's box in the woodshed was empty. Denny felt the blanket inside. It was cold and damp. The yellow moonlight showed that the food in Boot's dish hadn't been touched. "Boot! Boot! Come, Boot!" Denny called. He couldn't raise his voice too much—that would wake people up. He whistled. He waited a moment and whistled again. He stared at the gray bulk of the mountain and at the glittering stars of the Big Dipper poised above its rim. Suddenly the wild baying stopped.

Off to the right in the old pear orchard another sound took the place of the eerie baying. It was a faint rustling—as if something was moving slowly through the goldenrods and asters on the slope. Along the path that led up the slope a white patch appeared. It bobbed up and down, moved to the right, and vanished. "Boot! Boot!" Denny called softly. The white patch was the spot of white fur on Boot's chest—no doubt about that.

"Boot!" Denny whispered. The patch appeared again and wavered as if the dog were in doubt. Then it vanished. Denny ran up the hill and saw a clump of golden-rod waving. He heard a scratching sound. Boot was digging!

Denny pushed through the goldenrod and bent down over the dog. Boot grabbed something lying on the ground and started to run. Denny got a good grip on him and wrenched the something from his mouth. Boot looked up with a guilty air. Denny held up the object he'd taken from the dog. At first he couldn't imagine what it was. It seemed like some sort of bone and no more than that. Then Denny tumbled to the fact that it was a deer's foot and part of the leg bone. Had Boot been running deer with that crazy pack that had just then begun baying again high above? And had his pack brought down a deer and had Boot gorged himself to the point of spending the day dozing? It certainly looked that way. The other dogs were younger and faster. They were off after another deer while old Boot was chewing at the remains of one brought down on a previous night. These were the conclusions to which the facts seemed to point.

Boot was moving here and there on the hillside, following the trail of himself and his bone. Denny grabbed him by the collar. Once a dog has taken to running deer the fever isn't likely to leave his blood. He has to be kept tied up. That would have to be Boot's fate from now on until he calmed down. As Denny seized Boot the dog wagged his tail vigorously and gave a little squeak of pleasure. Poor Boot, Denny thought, he hasn't any idea of what's going to happen to him.

"Come on, Boot, come on!" Denny said softly. His voice echoed back to him, and something else seemed to come with it. Meech Hollow was a place with many little secrets of its own. For example, there were spots where a man could shout at the top of his lungs and have the sound swallowed up by the surrounding mountains. Someone a hundred yards away couldn't hear a sound.

But in the spot where Denny and Boot were it was just the opposite. Here every sound was amplified by the ridge running down the mountain and behind the house. Sounds bounced back as a ball does when it's thrown against a wall.

Denny straightened up. Someone was coming toward him. He saw a figure in white on the hillside below. It was Dad in his pajamas. He had been awakened when Denny called Boot and had come out to see what was going on.

Dad studied the deer foot as Denny explained. "This hasn't been chewed off by a dog," said Dad. "There are marks of a knife here—a good sharp knife. I wonder . . ."

"Was it deer-jackers?" Denny asked.

Dad nodded. "Yes, that's likely. The open season for

deer won't be here for quite a while. Whoever cut up this deer didn't have any right to do it. Probably one of those deer-jackers."

That was Denny's cue for pouring out all the story. Out came everything about the night before, about Ames and Uncle Frank. The two sat down on the stone wall at the bottom of the pear orchard as Denny talked and got a firm grip on the collar of the wriggling Boot. Once in a while Dad asked a question. Most of the time he listened and sometimes he nodded to show that he was following the story with interest. After a while he put a hand on Denny's arm. "Listen," he whispered as a dull hum broke through the rustling of trees and weeds around them. "Someone's coming up the Hollow."

A glow of light lit up the trees down the road. The light moved and danced, vanished, and appeared again a little closer. It burst into a big glare as a vehicle turned without a moment of hesitation into the orchard lane. "It's a jeep," Dad said soberly. The short distance between the two headlights and their height from the ground made that clear.

"It's the jackers again," Denny whispered.

The jeep slowed down. A long powerful beam of light shot from it and swept across the orchard.

"Duck!" Dad almost shouted as the beam approached. He and Denny dropped below the stone wall. The light passed by overhead and picked out the big, green pears

hanging on a tree ten feet away. The beam stopped moving like a glowing finger across the orchard. Denny saw what the finger was pointing at. It was three pairs of glitter, like six stars in the sky. They were the eyes of three deer standing still, fascinated by the mysterious light.

In his excitement Denny relaxed his hold on Boot's collar. The dog broke away. From somewhere among the weeds his indignant bark rang out. He bounced toward the jeep with his barking echoing mightily.

Whoever was in command of the jeep got the point at once. The light was switched off, leaving the Hollow plunged in what seemed for a moment like total blackness. Then the headlights of the jeep went on and with an urgent roar the jeep sped away. It clanked against a rock, then picked up speed and vanished.

Five minutes later Denny and his father were sitting in the kitchen drinking warm milk to chase away the chill of the night. Boot was cheerfully licking the dish in which Scampy the cat had had her dinner. "Well, there can't be any doubt now that there are deer-jackers around," said Dad. "The question is what to do about it." Dad had the kind of long face that went with his tall and thin body. He always had a serious look—except when he smiled. Now he looked almost grim.

"I'll call Jesse Ames in the morning," Denny said. "What else can we do?"

"Not much," Dad answered. Then he went on to

explain that even if a man has been seen jacking deer it might be hard to convict him in court. "There has to be pretty solid evidence. After all, even though we saw the lights of that jeep tonight, whoever was in it might have come here just for the ride. The light might have been turned on so that the people could admire the scenery."

Denny laughed.

"Well, how could anyone prove that wasn't their purpose?" Dad asked. "If a state trooper stops a car and finds a loaded rifle in it, then he has some evidence that a court will listen to. Or if he found a dead deer in the car. . . . But how can anybody tell who was here tonight or prove that he was trying to jack deer?"

"What about the place where the jeep bumped into a rock?" asked Denny. "Wouldn't some paint be scraped off and couldn't that be matched with the paint on the jeep?"

"I wouldn't count on a long shot like that," Dad said. "And even if you did locate the jeep that was here last night you still couldn't prove anything." Dad yawned and stretched his long arms. "I only hope it was nobody we know," he began slowly. "Suppose—" He paused and then continued, "Well, suppose we get to bed, Denny. It's late."

"Suppose"—the word buzzed in Denny's head as he got in bed. Had Dad begun to say, "Suppose it's some of our cousins from back of the mountain?" Well, the same possibility had been haunting Denny. But he pushed it aside and instead wondered what would happen when he called Jesse Ames. Would his clue lead to the breaking up of a vicious gang of deer-jackers? And would he become not exactly a hero but somebody sort of important because he'd done a fine job of investigating? The next day might answer these questions.

In the morning everything seemed to get snarled up. In the first place Denny's loss of sleep two nights running made it hard for him to get up at all. Mom's voice broke into his dreams: "Denny, *get up*. It's way past seven."

"O.K., just a minute," Denny muttered. He went back to dreaming again.

A few minutes later Mom was shouting up the stairs again. "Denny! If you don't get up right now you'll miss the bus!"

"O.K., Mom, I'm coming," Denny said and fell asleep again.

When he did get up Mom insisted he eat his breakfast before he called Jesse Ames. As he dialed the number Ames had given him, Mom was starting for the car. Hank was jumping up and down singing, "Hurry up, slowpoke, hurry up!"

Denny hurried so much that he dialed the wrong number and got old Mr. Kniffen out of bed. Mr. Kniffen was hard of hearing, so it took quite a while for Denny's explanation to sink in. When he did get the right number it wasn't Jesse Ames's house but the state police barracks on Round Pond Road. From the way the man at the other end repeated things after him it was plain that he was writing them down. He thanked Denny and asked him to call if anything further happened. And that was that.

Denny couldn't help feeling a little disappointed as he dashed out to the car. Dad and Mom and the state trooper he'd just talked with seemed to take things very calmly. Well, when he got home from school that afternoon he'd give the Hollow a good going-over. And he was sure he could find clues that would lead right to the jackers. He reached home that afternoon puffing hard from running part of the way up the hill from the bus stop.

Right away Denny saw that it wasn't going to be easy to get on the trail of the jackers. As he came into the house Mom sang out, "Hi, Denny. Have you got that paper on the nomadic Kurds written yet?"

Well, the answer was "No." And there were only a few days left to get it finished. Now it began to look as if the Kurds were going to join Mom and Dad and everybody else in keeping Denny from solving the mystery of the deer-jackers of Meech Hollow. When Miss Harvey had given the class a list of things to write about, all of them had seemed terrible until she came to the nomadic Kurds. As soon as Denny heard the words he sat up and felt excited. He didn't know what the nomadic Kurds were, but he said he'd write a paper about them. He kept repeating the words "nomadic Kurds, nomadic Kurds" all afternoon. Finally he got to the school library and found that there was hardly anything about the Kurds in all the books in the place. The librarian said she'd get some stuff for Denny and she did. It was all up in his room and he hadn't looked at it yet.

"Before you do anything else you'd better get at the Kurds," Mom said very firmly. "This isn't the kind of thing you can leave till the last minute."

Denny said there was lots of time, but when Mom pinned him down it turned out that there wasn't. "Think of how wonderful it will be to have it all over with," said Mom. "Denny, you get right at the Kurds before you do anything else."

Finally Denny said O.K., he'd work at the Kurds for an hour and get back at them after dark, and Mom said it was a bargain. Denny went to his room and read about how the Kurds are people who live in the Middle East and how they wander around in order to find good pastures for their sheep and goats. In the winter they stay in the valleys and in the summer they go up in the mountains. Denny wrote what he thought was a good first paragraph. Then he ran downstairs and called out to Mom. "Got a good start on the Kurds. I'll be back soon." And he raced outside before Mom could answer.

It was the time of year when you are surprised at how early the sun goes down. The sun wasn't very far above the top of Meech Mountain to the west of the Hollow. It looked very big and pale in the hazy sky. Already the side of the mountain was dark with shadow, and the shadow was sweeping relentlessly down the slope. Soon it would reach the valley and flow across it until it swallowed up the blue Berkshires on the other side. Then it would be night.

The thing Denny wanted to do first was to find out where Boot had gotten his deer's foot. Probably that would be somewhere on the big level place above the pear orchard. Denny charged up the mountain. He took the path worn by deer moving up and down in search of the various foods each season supplied. His eyes were on the ground in case any clue might be left: a cigarette butt of some strange Oriental brand, a footprint—

Something up ahead made Denny stop. It might have been a sound, it might have been a smell carried by the breeze, he didn't know. But when he stopped and looked he saw something that startled him. There was a man standing on the rocky ledge that marked the upper end of the pear orchard. He was a tall man with a pack on his back and a beard, and he seemed to be looking down into the valley as if admiring the view. But what was strangest about this stranger was that beside him was Boot, wagging his tail as if the man were an old friend. As Denny stared, a sound floated up from below. It was the rattling of a car up the lane. The rattling ended and a hearty voice floated up to Denny's ears. "Hi, Denny.

Come here a minute, will you?" It was the voice of Uncle Frank.

The man on the ledge turned his attention from the view to Uncle Frank and then to Denny. He vanished among the trees behind him. Denny stood like a statue. Should he follow the stranger? After all, he might have something to do with the sounds and lights he had heard and seen by night. He might be a deer-jacker. But at the same time Uncle Frank was calling him. Denny couldn't decide which way to go—up or down the mountain. It was his uncle who made up his mind for him. "Come on, Denny. I've got a surprise for you!"

Denny came to as if from a deep sleep. Slowly he started toward the red jeep standing in the twilight with Uncle Frank beside it.

3) A Present of Deer Meat

"YOUR SURPRISE is inside the jeep," said Uncle Frank as Denny approached. A dark-eyed lanky boy wearing a red hunting cap jumped out—he was the surprise. Uncle Frank was all smiles. The boy in the red cap was half smiles. Denny didn't smile for a second and then he joined in. His uncle explained.

"Your cousin Bert is going to stay with you and your folks for a little while. His dad and ma are going up north to see about a lumbering job—fellow up there plans to take out a lot of hard maples. You and Bert always got along fine—ought to have a good time together."

Bert was a year younger than Denny. But he was way ahead of him in knowing the ways of the woods and the animals living there. Bert never said much, but he didn't miss a single flicker of a chipmunk's eyelids. Sure, Denny was glad to see Bert—but not at the exact moment when the stranger was stalking away and the sun was setting. Besides, a dreadful thought came into his mind and wouldn't be driven out. Did Uncle Frank know that

Denny was on the trail of the deer-jackers and had he brought Bert there to keep an eye on him? Were the back-of-the-mountain folks involved in the deer-jacking?

"Hi," said Bert.

"Hi," said Denny.

Hank came up and said "Hi" too. He was dragging his little wagon after him. One wheel was off and he asked Denny to put it back on. Denny saw his chance and seized it. "Bert's very good at doing things like that, much better than I am. How about it, Bert? You can work at the bench in the woodshed. There's a light over it you can turn on."

There wasn't much Bert could do but say "Yes." And that was what he did. Uncle Frank roared off and Denny raced up the mountain. It was too late to try to track down the stranger, but there might be time to locate the place where Boot had found that piece of deer. He crossed the ledge where the stranger had stood a few minutes before and took a good look at the brushy field ahead. Something Bert had once said popped into his mind. "If you want to catch a trout you have to *be* a trout. If you want to catch a coon, you have to *be* a coon. That's what the old-time hunters used to say—and it's true."

Denny became a deer-jacker—in his imagination. He drove his jeep through the orchard below and swung his big flashlight across the place. Nothing doing. No sparkle of deer eyes there. Next he tackled the steep lane that led up to the spot where he was standing. All around were young sugar maples and sumacs. Deer had been there all right. The leaves of the sumacs had been nibbled off that summer when they were full of milky juice. Now the deer were nibbling them again, but at the soft tips of the sumac stems. An oak sapling had a long scar down its side where a buck had rubbed the bark away as he scraped the coating from his antlers.

Yes, this was a place that could easily attract deer-jackers. Along its edges were six-foot-high clumps of white pine trees, just right for a shy buck to hide behind. At one end a little brooklet tinkled away even after a dry summer, ready to give a drink to a thirsty deer. A swell of land shut off smells and sounds from the Meech house and all the world below.

Denny came back to earth. If the deer-jackers had been here, they would certainly have left some signs. Denny quickly hunted this way and that among the bushes, like a dog trying to find a partridge to set whirring into the sky for a hunter to fire at. Sure enough, he found the telltale marks of a jeep working its way among bushes and rocks toward the far end of the field. He followed the trail. As he came to where the clumps of pines stood he saw something moving among the tall goldenrod plants ahead. It couldn't be a rabbit, for it was too big and moved too steadily. Was it a porcupine? No, it was only Boot.

The dog seemed to be sniffing here and there in an

aimless way. He stopped sniffing and wagged his tail slowly in answer to Denny's whispered greeting. Denny felt sure that the source of the deer meat on which the dog had probably been gorging himself couldn't be far away.

As Denny plunged into the dark woods he called Boot to go with him. The dog hung back and then discreetly vanished. But Denny found out at once that he didn't need Boot's help. For once inside the woods his nose told him the body of a dead animal was not far away. In a few seconds he found the spot where the jackers had dressed their kill and left the parts they didn't want on the leafy carpet under an oak tree.

Denny stood in the dim woods and wondered. Why had the jackers been so careless? Most people who shot deer illegally picked up the deer as quickly as possible and beat it fast to dress the animals in some out-of-the-way building. But these fellows had acted almost as if they didn't care whether anybody saw them or not. That didn't seem to make sense because it might cost them as much as a thousand dollars a deer if they were caught and convicted.

Denny headed for home. He felt sure now that whoever had shot the three or four deer which had been dressed in the woods, they weren't folks from back of the mountain; *they* had too much sense to do things that way.

Anger at the jackers built up inside Denny as he

watched Boot cheerfully trotting home. Boot had been a fine respectable dog. The jackers had made an outlaw of him by tempting him to feast on deer they had killed. Maybe Boot had met the dogs in the pack that had bayed up the mountain the night before. Boot was old—but not too old to join the pack if only now and then. Denny had decided the night before that Boot would have to be kept tied up for a while, but he hadn't followed through. Once he got back to the house he'd see that Boot was securely chained. He and the dog were old friends. One of his earliest memories was of Boot as a wriggling puppy chewing up everything in sight. They'd been together ever since. It wouldn't do to let the dog get in trouble and become an outlaw—not old Boot.

Down the hill through the old pear orchard—that took only a minute. There was the house ahead, its windows glowing because night had almost arrived. Against one of the living room windows stood Bert with his face turned toward the mountain. Bert raised an arm and pointed to the right. "Did you see that bear?" he asked softly. "He came over the hill a little while ago and headed that way." Bert was pointing toward the spur of Meech Mountain, which old-timers called The Beehive.

"This time of year some bears will eat things they wouldn't touch in the summer," said Bert. "Guess they're not too particular what they fatten up on for the winter. Maybe this bear comes down to chew at a deer somebody's shot and left in the woods. He'd come down from way up the mountain at dusk, eat for a while, and then go back up again."

"I didn't see any bear," Denny answered slowly. But he didn't tell Bert what he had seen. How was he going to keep on the trail of the jackers with Bert's sharp eyes right behind him—or maybe a few steps ahead? He was even more worried when Bert said casually, "I think I'll take a look around pretty soon. I'd like to find whatever's bringing that bear down. I'll bet it's a dead deer lying in the woods."

"Um-hum," said Denny. Jesse Ames had said that and it had struck Denny as a fine expression to use. It sounded as if you knew a lot more than you were letting on. He tried it again, "Um-hum." Bert stared at him in the twilight. Was he impressed? It looked like it.

As the two boys walked to the door Denny did some fast thinking. If there was a bear fooling around with the deer carcasses, that might explain some of Boot's odd actions. The dog was wary of bears. Once when Uncle Frank had shot a bear up the mountain and brought him down past the house Boot had cowered and run into the house as soon as he got a whiff of bear. Maybe on some nighttime wandering the dog had had a brush with a bear. He might have decided that a bear was one creature he couldn't handle. Boot was brave—but not too brave.

It's funny how two things can go on at the same time

inside a person—that was the thought that struck Denny. Here he was thinking about bears and Boot and at the same time he was wondering in a dreamy way whether it mightn't be a good idea to tell Bert everything. After all, there wasn't a chance of keeping anything from him. He was smart as a steel trap, as Grandpa used to say.

Denny stood with a hand on the kitchen doorknob and talked: of the strange things by night in the Hollow, Uncle Frank, Jesse Ames—everything. And once he'd done that he felt better. He felt free as a balloon that has thrown out its ballast and is soaring into the sky. Bert just nodded and said, "Yes." Maybe he was trying to make out that he'd known everything all along. And of course maybe he had.

"I guess we'd better bury what's left of those deer," Denny said. And right away he knew that was a dumb thing to say. That free balloon was making him talk nonsense. Of course he couldn't touch the deer. It might be needed for evidence, for one thing. For another, the law said that nobody but a game protector could touch a dead deer lying in the woods. It was his job to bury it if it was past being sent to some public institution, like the county home, to be eaten.

Bert pointed out all these things in a quiet voice. He said that plenty had been happening lately on the deer-jacker front. An old man named Calvin Pease had been wounded by some jackers in his woodlot on Bull Hill.

Ames was working on the case. He wouldn't have the time to bury any deer innards for a while. But trying it themselves would be a crazy thing to do.

Denny felt his face turning hot. How could he have made such a dumb remark? Instead of going inside with Bert he turned to the woodshed and tied Boot to an iron ring fastened to the wall. He used an old chain that had been hanging on a nail ever since he could remember. Boot didn't mind at all. He took it as a kind of joke and wagged his tail as if to show he got the point. Denny petted Boot. He felt better.

Once inside the house the very first thing that happened was that Mom stopped stirring the Bavarian beef stew and sang out, "How about those nomadic Kurds, Denny?"

Denny said after all it was Friday night and he had all weekend to take care of the Kurds; why rush things? Then he looked at Bert, expecting him to pour out all kinds of stuff about the Kurds. But Bert just said he didn't know a thing about the Kurds, and who or what they were. He said wasn't it wonderful what a lot there was that a person didn't know a thing about and the Kurds sounded interesting.

Denny lit right into the Kurds. He talked about them all through dinner. He was going strong when Mom served the chocolate layer cake and he was talking so much he got a crumb down the wrong way and coughed himself out of talking for a while. He was still coughing occasionally when Boot seemed to join in outside and then burst out barking. It wasn't long before what Boot was barking at walked into the kitchen. It was Uncle Frank. But this wasn't the same Uncle Frank that Denny had eaten an apple with the day before. He seemed shrunken and smaller and his face looked saggy. No doubt about it, something was bothering him.

"Anybody seen my boy Bill?" he asked right off.

Mom was awfully polite. Sometimes Denny didn't see the sense of it and this was one of those times. Instead of answering the question Mom fussed about getting Frank to sit down. She offered him a slice of cake and he said, "No, the way I feel it would be like eating a bale of hay—not that your chocolate cake isn't the best this side of Poughkeepsie." Mom said no, she hadn't seen Bill since the church supper last week, and Dad, Denny and Bert said the same. Denny asked what was the matter with Bill.

"He's gone!" cried Uncle Frank. "There were a couple of state troopers around just now wanting to know where he was." Uncle Frank got up from his chair. Denny noticed how the light from the ceiling hit his face and made it look all silver like dew on the grass because he hadn't shaved that day. Uncle Frank stamped his foot until the dishes on the table rattled.

"Why can't they ever forget it!" he exclaimed. "Somebody's been singing the same song to the troopers and that's why they're checking up on Bill."

"Old Billy Meech he had a gun," sang Uncle Frank. He stamped with one foot. The dishes on the table rattled. "They can't forget about it and it happened seventy-five years ago. Whenever anything goes wrong in the mountains, they go blaming it on the Meeches. Now they act as if my Bill had something to do with Cal Pease being shot."

Mom was indignant. "Of course Bill didn't have anything to do with it," she exclaimed. "A nice boy like Bill!" Mom said hadn't Bill gone out after those woodchucks in the upper pasture in Yankee Hollow? He was great at shooting woodchucks. Uncle Frank said no, Bill hadn't even taken his gun.

There was one thing had him worried, Uncle Frank said as he sat down. Bill hadn't taken hold of things since he left high school. He'd worked here and there in garages and on farms, but he didn't know just what he wanted to do with himself. Pretty soon he'd be drafted into the Army, and after that he'd settle down all right. But right now he was a little wild at times. Didn't know just when he'd be called up for the Army and that helped make him restless.

Only the other day, said Uncle Frank, a couple of fellows were talking with Bill and he'd heard Bill say in a joking way that there was real money in jacking deer. Bill was only fooling, of course, but after those troopers left him, Uncle Frank got to thinking that maybe Bill knew something about the jackers. Maybe he'd seen something or recognized somebody. . . .

Uncle Frank slowly pulled himself out of his chair. "Well, I've got to go hunting for Bill," he said. "Maybe he's in trouble. Maybe it's like they say and there's devils loose in the Catskills."

Dad smiled and said he didn't take much stock in that talk about devils. "I'll go along and help you, Frank," he added. "I'm not working tomorrow so I don't mind a bit."

Denny jumped up and asked if he could go too. Dad said he couldn't. He'd be really useful if he stayed home and took care of things there with Bert's help. "Watch out for those devils," he said, "and if you see anything funny going on outside don't go out after it. Your place is right here in the house—understand?"

"Yessir," Denny and Bert answered together.

Bert was always quiet, but he was quieter than ever that evening. Once he started saying there was something he wanted to tell Denny, and then he said never mind, it could wait. When the two boys played checkers before going to bed, Bert lost—and that was something that had never happened before because Bert was a smart player.

After Denny had gotten in bed Bert said there was something he just had to talk about with somebody. He sat down on the edge of Denny's bed. "I know a place where Bill might have gone," he began. "It's this place he fixed up on Sawtooth Mountain last spring. He was planning to use it during the hunting season." Bert's face lit up with enthusiasm as he talked about the place. It wasn't any ordinary shack in the woods. Bill had found a place near the mountaintop where a big slice of cliff had pulled away from the topmost ledge thousands of years ago and stayed there instead of crashing down into the upper part of Yankee Hollow. Between the piece that had pulled away and the ledge there was a place like a big room without a roof. Bill had used a lot of stuff to make a roof so that from above it looked like a tangle of dead branches. Inside he had a stove and beds and other such things.

Denny interrupted to ask why Bert hadn't told Uncle Frank about the place. Bert said Bill had asked him not to and he'd promised. He wanted to have that place be just his and nobody else's. It was his secret hideout. Bert knew about it because he'd helped Bill haul the stuff up there with ropes. You had to climb right up the cliff— that was the only way to reach the hideout. You couldn't see the place from anywhere, not even from a plane except if there was a fire in the stove, and Bill didn't have one unless there were clouds hanging around the top of Sawtooth to hide the smoke.

"All right," said Denny, "let's go to the hideout to-morrow and see if Bill is there. If he isn't you won't have to tell anybody about the place. If he is all we have to do is to tell him people are looking for him. After that he can do what he wants about it."

Bert nodded enthusiastically. "You're right," he said. "That's an O.K. idea. I've been thinking and thinking and I couldn't figure out what to do, but you got it right off."

Denny almost blushed at this praise. It encouraged him to ask a question that had been bothering him. "Bert," he asked earnestly, "does Bill or any of the other people in Yankee Hollow have anything to do with all this deer-jacking?"

Bert didn't hesitate a moment. He shook his head vigorously. "No," he said, "I've never seen or heard anything to make me think they have anything at all to do with it. Bill—or anybody else."

Denny felt as if some heavy guy sitting on his shoulders had just jumped off. He'd never admitted how much he'd worried about the possibility that the back-of-the-mountain people were mixed up in deer-jacking. What Bert said seemed to settle that. The minute Denny lay down again he went right to sleep.

Later that night—Denny never knew just when— Boot barked and rattled his chain furiously. Everybody in the house woke up. Denny and Bert looked out their window. A streak of clouds covered the moon and made it too dark to see anything. Denny thought he heard a sound like footsteps on the drive, but Boot's barking made it hard to be sure.

Hank woke up and wailed. The hall light went on as Mom galloped to Hank's rescue. Denny and Bert raced downstairs. Mom called out that she thought she'd heard something moving on the porch. She asked Denny to take a look while she got Hank quieted down. As Denny made for the front door Scampy the cat dashed in front of him and down he went in order to keep from stepping on her. Bert tumbled down on top of him. It was all pretty crazy. Mom came running down to see what was going on while Hank wailed. Outside, Boot's barking got louder and angrier.

By the time Denny got up and opened the door there was nothing outside but a carton sitting on the stone floor. It was the kind of carton that packages of Vitasnaps, the power-plus cereal, comes in. On top was a sheet of paper from a composition book. It was fastened down with an old rusty nail and there was something lettered on it. Denny held the paper under the hall light and read it aloud:

DEAR FRIENDS,

This is for minding your own business. There's more where this comes from if you go on minding your business and sleep good nights.

As Denny read the message Bert pulled the carton inside. He took out a package neatly wrapped in wax paper. "Deer meat," he explained after a quick look.

"It's been cut by a real butcher. Whoever did this knew his business. It looks as if the jackers are trying to bribe us to keep quiet."

Denny said the jackers must be dumb to try a raw thing like that. Bert said it wasn't so dumb; it had worked with plenty of people. It made people choose sides. If they accepted the meat, they were with the jackers. If they didn't, they were on the side of the law. Old Cal Pease had refused the deer meat and they'd tried to kill him the next day.

Mom said there wouldn't be any two ways about it—the Meeches wouldn't let that jacked meat inside their house.

"Put it back where you got it, boys," she ordered.

Bert stood with the deer meat in his hands and said it wasn't so easy. "Deer meat is perishable in this kind of weather. You put it out on the porch and it'll be a smelly mess pretty soon—if a dog doesn't haul it away. There's sure to be a cloud of flies around it once the sun gets going in the morning. And the jackers wouldn't ever come back to get their meat."

Mom said she got the point. In the morning she was going to the new Sooperdooper Market near the Spacemaster plant because they were giving out double stamps. That would take her past Jesse Ames's house. She could leave the meat there. It could stay in her refrigerator overnight.

With that settled, everybody, including Boot, quieted

down and started to get back to sleep. Then once again Boot exploded into barking and Hank wailed. Everybody jumped out of bed and ran downstairs, with Scampy ducking in and out among their legs as she ran to take refuge under Hank's bed. When Boot's barking softened up, there was a roaring outside. "It's just Dad coming back!" Denny exclaimed in relief.

It was Dad all right. And a rather worried Dad. He and Frank had gone everywhere they thought Bill might be but they hadn't found a trace of him. Poor Uncle Frank had gotten so tired he began to mutter that those devils loose in the Catskills were after Bill. When he began to talk like that, Dad took him home and put him to bed. His wife wasn't there. She had gone on an overnight bus trip to Albany with her lodge, the Eastern Star. A couple of Frank's cousins were keeping up the search—Enoch and old Sam, the one with the beard, not young Sam.

"A funny thing happened as I came up the Hollow Road," Dad said. "Near that clump of red pines I thought I saw headlights ahead, but when I got there it was as dark as the inside of a pocket. I stopped and got out of the jeep. I didn't hear or see anything. But I'm sure I smelled the smoke of a cigar. It was a strong smell as if the man smoking was right beside me. I'll take a look tomorrow if I can. Maybe somebody ducked into one of those wood roads that branch off near the pines."

"It was the deer-jackers going down and trying to escape being spotted," Denny explained. He and Bert and Mom told Dad about the deer meat and the note.

Dad's face became very serious. "This is getting pretty bad," he said. "Why I just heard more about Cal Pease. He set some deer meat he found on his doorstep along the road with a note saying he didn't want it. He was working in his woodlot the next day and a bullet whizzed over his head. The second bullet sent him to the hospital."

All the group, crowded into the little hall with its cheerful flowered wallpaper, looked at each other and all of them felt a threat in the silent darkness outside. Now they knew that they were bystanders in a dangerous game. It was no longer a matter of just hearing an occasional jeep coming up the road by night, or a shot now and then echoing from Meech Mountain at dawn. Dad said he'd heard that a ruthless big-city gang was trying to organize all the scattered deer-jacking that had been going on here and there into a big and profitable business. The state troopers and the game protectors were working hard to crack the gang, but people said they found it tough going. But until that gang was out of business, everybody in the Hollow would have to be mighty careful, especially at night.

At this moment Denny asked Dad if he and Bert could go up Sawtooth Mountain in the morning. Dad seemed a little surprised and then he smiled. "I don't know any mountain in the Catskills where you're less likely to meet a deer or a jacker than on Sawtooth," he said. "There's nothing there for a deer to eat. I guess it's a safer place than the Hollow. Sure, you go ahead. But get back before dark and stay high on the mountain. Keep out of the hollows where the deer are."

As Denny and Bert were getting into bed again Dad looked into their room. "Plan to go up Meech Mountain and along Beech Ridge to the top of Sawtooth?" he asked.

"That's the best way, I guess," Denny said.

Dad nodded. "Yes, it's the quickest—and in these times the safest. Well, have fun and keep your eyes open and watch out for those devils." Dad smiled and went on to his room.

"I don't get this stuff about devils," Denny complained to Bert. "What's it all about?"

Bert yawned and stretched as he sat on the edge of his bed. "Joe Woolsome, that man on the radio station in Benton, keeps talking about them," he said, "but you know what wild ideas he gets sometimes. Well, the last time I listened to his local news broadcast—that was yesterday—he told about some woman over in Methodist Center claiming she'd seen a devil."

"Where's Methodist Center?" Denny asked as he got under the covers.

"Oh, it's on the backside of Sawtooth Mountain," Bert replied.

Denny wouldn't have showed how startled he was for anything. He pulled himself together enough to say "Um-hum" in a very good imitation of Jesse Ames trying not to give away anything at all.

4) The Bearded Man

NOBODY IN the Meech house wanted to get up the next morning. Even Mom overslept and didn't call Denny until eight instead of at seven as she'd promised. When she did rouse Denny he went right back to sleep again. It wasn't until Mom called him at eight-thirty that Denny hauled himself out of bed and began getting Bert going. Bert was quick enough when he was awake, but he was a slow starter in the morning. Denny had to pull him out of bed before he came to.

While the boys ate breakfast Mom fixed a lunch for them to put in their packs. Bert stood around with his pack on his back while Denny hunted for his camera—he was determined to take it with him. But he couldn't find it. He looked all over. Bert kept calling him to hurry. When he found the camera at last there wasn't any film in it, so he couldn't take it anyway. He was cross as he started away from the house.

In the woodshed Boot was jumping up and down with joy when he saw that a hike was beginning. Denny had always taken him along, but that was not to be this

time. As the boys went up the Hollow they could hear
Boot's voice imploring them to come back and unchain
him so that he could go with them. Denny couldn't help
feeling mean about leaving Boot. As he walked he
kicked every fallen branch to get the meanness out of his
system.

Denny had climbed Meech Mountain so often that
he had worked out a fine way of getting to the top. He
hadn't marked the trail he used, but he could follow it
without hesitation at all seasons. But when he and Bert
came to the brook which they had to cross at the point
where the mountain began to rise steeply, Bert had an
idea. It would be simpler to follow the brook bed this
time, he explained. The water was very low. That would
make it possible to go from rock to rock up the brook
bed. It would be almost like climbing stairs, and there
would be no laurel bushes or scrub oaks to battle. The
fact that Bert was right made it all the harder for Denny
to give in, but he took a deep breath and said "O.K."

By that time Denny felt pretty low. So much had gone
wrong that morning. He couldn't help thinking about all
kinds of dismal things, including that paper on the nomadic Kurds—and the Kurds promptly came to his
rescue.

"Bert," Denny called out, "let's pretend we're nomadic Kurds on their way to their summer pastures."

Bert, looking a little baffled, asked what Denny meant.

"The Kurds go off to their pastures in a long line they

call a *baro-dan*. There's a guy playing a flute up ahead and all kinds of sheep and goats and things tagging along. Everybody's singing and keeping the animals from getting away."

Denny started singing "Yankee Doodle." Bert joined in and the two raced from rock to rock up the mountain. Pretty soon Denny felt so much like a nomadic Kurd that he could almost feel the cartridge belt across his chest and the turban on his head. When he scrambled up on the ledge that marked the top of Meech Mountain, Denny gasped that he wished he'd timed it; they must have set a record, thanks to the Kurds. Bert agreed but he thought it was taking the brook bed that did it. They didn't argue; they were too much out of breath.

In a few minutes the boys were heading across the flat top of the mountain toward the long ridge that led to Sawtooth. Off to the left they could see the mass of the mountain dark with evergreens. There were the three projecting rocks which gave the mountain its name, although Uncle Frank said it should have been called Sawteeth because it had three teeth. Bert pointed toward the third of the sawteeth. "See—there's the hideout on top of that gray rock near the top."

Denny stared. He put one hand on his forehead to keep the stiff mountaintop breeze from blowing his hair in his eyes. All he could see was rock and trees. There was no hint that Bill's hideout was tucked away high on the mountain. As Denny stared he saw a dark dot moving along one side of the gray rock. "Look, Bert," he called to Bert. "What's that moving up the rock?"

Bert looked and caught a glimpse of a dark spot moving for a moment. Then it vanished. "It could be Bill," he said. "It looks as if he's there all right. He might have been climbing back to the hideout after going down for water. There's a spring in the place, but likely it would be dry now. Come on, let's hurry."

The boys settled down to the job of getting to the hideout as quickly as possible. They didn't waste any time in talking—already it was around noon. They raced down the mountain, jumping from rock to rock until they came to the beginning of Beech Ridge. From there on the going was easy for a while, but soon patches of tangled bushes and stretches of rough broken rock slowed them down. Both the boys were hot and tired by the time they came to the spring that seeped out from beneath a mossy ledge. There they rested a moment and filled their canteens for the long dry pull ahead.

As Denny started off from the spring a long tough stem of a shinhopple bush caught his leg and pulled him to the ground. He was up in a moment, feeling unhurt. But later on that fall was to play a part in the troubles of the day.

It seemed half a day—actually it was only an hour and a half—before the two boys came to the end of Beech Ridge and began climbing Sawtooth. "This is the hardest way to get up," Bert pointed out, "but it's the quickest. Look down there. You can see how Bill gets to his hideout. You can trace the wood road that goes along the Yankee Kill from his place and ends up close to the bottom of the third tooth."

Denny looked down at sunny Yankee Hollow and recognized the little narrow farms of his back-of-the-mountain cousins strung out one after another along the stream. And highest of all was Uncle Frank's with the new metal roof on his barn glittering in the sunlight. All around were the dark woods and ragged ledges, which made the fields and houses below look as if they might be swallowed up at any moment by the great flood of trees and rocks that surged around them.

Quickly Yankee Hollow vanished as a shoulder of Sawtooth Mountain shut off the view. Denny and Bert toiled upward under the broiling sun with only Bert's knowledge of the mountain to keep them on the right track. After half an hour they stopped climbing and began moving along a narrow ledge with dizzy views of Yankee Hollow coming and going beneath.

"Almost there," Bert panted. "Another ten minutes and we'll make it." He scrambled hastily over an expanse of smooth rock which pitched steeply toward the valley. Bert was leading. Denny, coming up from behind, saw him suddenly freeze where he stood. As Denny joined Bert he too froze and stared down the side of the mountain. At the base of a cliff a short distance ahead was a kind of clearing with a huge spreading beech tree on the opposite side—a tree which dwarfed everything around it. But it wasn't the size of the tree which startled Denny and Bert. It was the six deer carcasses which they saw hanging from a low branch.

"That's the place where you start climbing up to Bill's hideout," Bert said slowly as if he didn't believe what he was saying. "It's the exact spot."

Denny slumped down on the ledge. So Bill was jacking deer after all. But how could he do such a thing? He was such a nice friendly fellow, always saying little things to make people laugh. Now he was right in the middle of the network of crime that was spreading over the mountains. If it had been only one deer you might have thought Bill had given in to temptation at a weak moment. But six . . . That looked as if Bill hadn't been kidding when Uncle Frank heard him talking about how much money there was in the deer-jacking business.

Bert just stared on at those six deer carcasses. "Let's go back, Denny," he said at last. "I don't want to see any more of this. Come on." He turned to retrace his steps to Meech Hollow.

Then Denny spoke up. "No, we've got to go on. After all Bill may have some explanation—"

"Such as?" Bert asked bitterly.

Denny couldn't think of anything to suggest. "We've got to know what's happening before we walk out on Bill," he said slowly. That was it—you couldn't condemn anybody, especially a cousin, until you were positive. You had to do everything you could think of first so that you could be sure you weren't making a dreadful mistake. While Denny was thinking, that silly tune drifted into his head:

> *Old Billy Meech he had a gun,*
> *He shot a deer and then he run. . . .*

Yes, things looked bad enough for Bill. And for Uncle Frank. And for all the back-of-the-mountain people—unless Denny and Bert could find an explanation that would clear Bill. "Come on, Bert, let's go to the hideout and see Bill," Denny said firmly.

Bert still stared at those deer carcasses. He glanced at Denny and said, "O.K." He followed Denny down the steep slope without saying another word. Ten minutes later the boys were standing in the clearing where the deer carcasses gently swayed as the branch on which they hung moved in the afternoon breeze.

Bert pointed to a broad and rough crack in the cliff above. "That's the way to the hideout," he whispered. "It's easier than it looks. You go straight up to where that little pine tree sticks out and then you swing left— Look, let's just call Bill first."

Denny went along with that. "Hey, Bill!" he shouted. The two shouted together. Then they waited for a reply.

A chipmunk whistled from a spruce stump nearby. From somewhere far away the breeze brought the lazy cawing of a crow. But that was all. "Maybe Bill's asleep," Bert suggested. "Let's try again."

"Hey, Bill!" The shout echoed against the cliff—*Bill-bill-bill*.

This time an answer came. There was a sharp crack and a nasty whine. A white streak two feet long appeared on a big rock to show where a rifle bullet had plowed its way through the dark lichens. Denny dashed toward the base of the cliff to get out of range of whoever was firing from the hideout. Bert followed.

The boys waited tensely, but there was no second shot. Not a sound came from the hideout above. The chipmunk went on giving his whistle—that was all that could be heard.

"Listen. I thought I heard a dog barking," said Denny.

For a full minute the two listened and then Denny shook his head.

"Bill's crazy to jack deer in the first place," said Bert. "He's even crazier to shoot at us. But he wouldn't be crazy enough to keep a dog up there to give him away. He'd never do a thing like that."

As Bert spoke, something zigzagged through Denny's mind like a flash of lightning on a black night. He grabbed Bert's arm. "That's not Bill up there," he whispered. "It's somebody else. I think the gang of jackers have taken over Bill's hideout."

Bert gave Denny a quick glance. "I wondered what that thing was doing over there," he whispered. He pointed to a crumpled cigarette package. "Bill doesn't smoke."

"But where's Bill, then?" Denny asked. It wasn't pleasant to think of what might have happened. Bill overpowered and lying bound and gagged in the hideout above . . . All kinds of dreadful possibilities elbowed their way into Denny's mind.

Bert shook his head as he looked at Denny. He was having the same thoughts. "I don't know what to do," he said. "I guess we'd better head down the Hollow and get help. If we can get out from under this cliff without being shot."

Denny had a better plan. "I'll sneak along the base of the cliff until I can get out of range of the hideout. Then I'll take the wood road down to Uncle Frank's. He finally had a telephone put in when Aunt Jessie was sick last spring. And you're much better in the woods than I am. Could you sneak up the mountain to a place where you could keep an eye on the hideout?"

"There's a good place near where we first saw those deer. I could see anybody coming or going to the hideout from there. And they couldn't see me—not unless they knew exactly where to look."

"O.K., then I'll—" Denny stopped as a rustling sound came from the right. With all their senses on the alert both boys braced themselves for whatever might be coming. And out of the bushes raced old Boot, tail wagging, and barking and yelping with joy.

"Stop that, Boot," Denny ordered sharply. The dog cringed at this unexpected welcome. He whimpered softly. His tail wagged again as Denny stroked his head.

It was plain that the dog had broken loose, for a bit of the rusty old chain which Denny had used to tie him was still dangling from his collar. What wasn't so plain was what to do next, for it would be impossible to move without Boot giving them away. Encouraged by Denny's hand on his head, Boot broke again into a series of joyful yelps. Denny ended that by the simple means of holding the dog's muzzle closed. "We'd better get out of here fast," Denny whispered. "If whoever is in the hideout goes hunting for us, he wouldn't have any trouble finding us now. Come on!"

With Denny crouched down and holding the short chain on Boot's collar, the boys made their way along the base of the cliff in the direction from which they had come. They couldn't help moving noisily, for hanging on to Boot made it hard for Denny to avoid sounding in general rather like a young elephant crashing through the jungle. But there was no further sound or movement from the hideout. Finally they rounded a bulge in the cliff which shut off the view of any possible observers in the hideout or near it.

To the right the Yankee Kill ran through a grove of tall hemlocks. The softness of the carpet of brown needles beneath and the gentle sound of the running water made Denny and Bert realize how tired and thirsty they had become. They stretched out on the ground and unpacked the lunches Mom had packed—it seemed a week ago that she had bustled around the kitchen and asked which they wanted, liverwurst or bologna sandwiches. When he'd eaten, Denny cut a strap that wasn't really necessary from his pack and fastened it to the bit of chain dangling from Boot's collar. Now he would be able to stand up as he and Boot traveled together down the Hollow toward Uncle Frank's.

"O.K." Denny stood up and stretched. Bert slung on his pack, smiled at Denny, and headed toward Sawtooth Mountain. Denny watched him with admiration as he moved from beneath the hemlocks into the rough country beyond. He walked steadily and apparently without effort, yet in almost complete silence. Not a crackling of a twig or a rustling of the leaves of a bush came to Denny's ears. There was no doubt about it—Bert was a born woodsman. He would surely get to his observation post without being seen or heard by the mysterious occupant of the hideout.

With Denny it was very different. The woods were full of squirrels and chipmunks—there hadn't been so many for years. Right now they were busily gathering beechnuts to stow away for the winter. And if there was anything in this world that got Boot stirred up it was a squirrel or chipmunk minding his own business in the fall woods. He would want to bark up every tree that held a squirrel. Yet if Denny let Boot do that, the dog would give away the fact that he was going for help. Whoever was in the hideout hadn't made a sound since that rifle was fired, but that didn't mean that both Denny and Bert might not be under close observation. If the man or men in the hideout were part of the big-city jacking gang, they were the kind who wouldn't miss a trick.

It wasn't too easy to move through the woods with Boot on a leash. Sometimes the dog chose one side of a tree he was approaching and Denny the other. Every once in a while a frantic tugging at the strap in his hand told Denny that Boot's nose had picked up a hot squirrel scent. Often Boot simply refused to move from the base of a tree until the squirrel overhead had made his way over a bridge of high branches to another tree.

Boot was a bright dog and he soon made it clear that an old dog will quickly learn what his master expects him to do. He was soon passing trees on the same side as Denny—most of the time. He was passing up squirrels after only a second of struggling with temptation. Denny felt encouraged to move faster and began to think of turning to the right and joining the wood road that led to Uncle Frank's. Everything had gone well. It ought to be safe to come out of the rough country and take to the road now.

As Denny turned from the bank of the Yankee Kill he was brought to an abrupt halt by an unexpected smell. Someone, very close by, was frying bacon!

Denny and Boot were standing in a patch of wood

nettles. They sidled out of the patch. Denny crouched down behind a rock and took a firm grip on Boot's collar. He studied the situation with care. The wind was blowing up Yankee Hollow, which meant that the bacon frier was downstream—and only a short distance at that, judging from the intensity of the smell. Denny rose and peered through the long-legged laurel bushes to the south. He thought he caught a glimpse of something— he moved carefully this way and that. Then he saw the kind of camping picture you might see on the cover of an outdoor magazine, framed by the laurel's shaggy legs. A nice little tent was pitched on a smooth hemlock needle carpet. In front of it was a fireplace with a frying pan on it. Beside the fireplace lay a pack. An arrow-straight beam of sunlight caught the smoke curling from the fire and made a blue stripe slanting at the brown needles. From close to the tent a chipmunk appeared in the patch of sunlight and set Boot quivering with eagerness to be at him.

"Quiet, Boot," Denny whispered. Did this tent have something to do with the deer-jackers? Denny asked himself. Or was this the camp of some innocent city man who had blundered into this nook of the Catskills where jackers were at work and—if you believed those tales— devils were loose. Boot began struggling harder. He shook off Denny's hand from his muzzle and burst into a full-blown bark. At that moment Denny saw the side of the tent wriggling. The flap opened and out came the

same bearded man he had seen silhouetted against the mountain in Meech Hollow.

Just why he acted as he did, Denny never knew. If he had used his head he would have known better than to give in to the wave of panic that swept over him. As it was he jumped up and raced away from his hiding place, dragging Boot after him. For about a hundred feet all went well. Then a shout came in pursuit from the camp: "Hello, hello—*Hello!*"

Boot stopped abruptly. His strap crossed Denny's legs, but Denny didn't realize that. He felt as if someone had tackled him from behind. He felt himself pitching forward as a sharp pain shot up his leg.

The next thing Denny knew was that he was lying on his back looking up at a bearded face and a cloud of blue smoke floating among hemlock branches.

"Just be quiet now," came from the bearded face. "Everything's all right. You just fainted slightly—that's all."

An insect was buzzing near Denny's eyes. Above him Boot's face appeared. It looked enormous. The dog's tongue popped out and gave Denny a reassuring lick.

"You can take my word for it—you're all right," spoke the bearded face. "You were pretty lucky at that. You might have hit that forehead of yours on a rock. But fainting is nothing to worry about. It can happen to the toughest men. A shock, a fright, and out you go."

Up to that moment Denny had taken things as they

came. It was just as if he'd been born again and was starting life from the beginning. But suddenly everything flashed into his mind in one huge and disturbing picture: Bill, Bert keeping watch over the hideout, the jackers. . . .

Denny sat up and felt a dull pain shooting down his right leg. "I have to get going," he said. "We have to find Bill—" Denny stopped as he stood unsteadily on his feet. Who was this man he was talking to—the man he had seen before and who seemed to know Boot? Was he one of the deer-jackers?

"You mentioned Bill," said the bearded man. "There are plenty of Bills in this world. Which one are you looking for?"

Denny gave the bearded man a curious look. He saw a kindly smile playing over his tanned face. The man didn't look wicked or dangerous. In fact he looked trustworthy. "Bill Meech," said Denny.

"Oh, Bill Meech. He's doing very well, I assure you. You needn't worry about him. But there isn't much you can do for Bill or anyone else right now. You must have banged your leg a few hours ago and your fall made it worse. You seem to have a little sprain that will keep you from doing much running around for a day or two."

Denny took a step and again the pain shot down his leg. "It must have been that shinhopple I tripped on this morning," he said. "It made my leg feel a little funny, but I didn't pay any attention—"

"Very treacherous stuff, that shinhopple," said the bearded man. "Lovely white flowers in the spring, lovely red berries later on. But those slinky stems—they lie in wait in the woods and wrap themselves around human legs and trip up innocent hikers. Some people call it hobblebush. That's a good name, too. But it's really a viburnum. Maybe you know that?"

Denny smiled. Mom had given him books about trees and plants on his birthdays and at Christmas, and he'd studied them. "Viburnum *alnifolium*—that's its name," he said.

The bearded man seemed delighted. "Fine!" he exclaimed. "You and I are going to get along very well, I can see. Imagine you knowing that!"

Denny gave the man a sharp look. "Are you a teacher?" he blurted out.

The bearded man laughed. "Only in the way we're all teachers," he said. "Don't all of us teach each other things as we go through this world? For example, a little while ago you taught me that it's possible for a boy to race through the woods with a dog on the end of a homemade leash and think he can get away without a smash-up. No, I'm a doctor."

Denny stepped forward. "I can't waste any time. I've got to get down to Uncle Frank's—right away." He stumbled and the bearded man caught him firmly by the arm.

"Look here," said the man. "There's certainly something on your mind. You have some errand to run. All right, let's make a deal. You're in no state to go dashing through the woods, but you could guard my camp very nicely while I run that errand for you. How about it?"

While the man was talking he'd been rummaging in a bag which he took from his pack. He opened a bottle and shook out a small white pill. "Here," he said, "you take this and you won't mind that leg so much. Here's some water to help it down."

Denny stared at the little pill lying in the hollow of his hand. He knew nothing of the man who had given it to him except what the man had told him. For all he knew the man might be part of the deer-jacking gang. The pill might even be poison. Yet in the few minutes he had known the bearded man Denny had come to believe he could trust him. He put the pill in his mouth and swallowed it.

5) *Trapped in the Hideout*

THE BEARDED MAN seemed to be one of those people who can get a dozen things done all at once. He put his frying pan back on the fire, added a couple of eggs to his bacon, exchanged his moccasins for boots, and at the same time led Denny into telling far more than he had intended about the deer-jackers, Bert, the hideout, and his adventures in Meech Hollow.

After he had fed Denny and himself and tied Boot to a sapling, he set off to bring help. It wasn't until after Denny had watched the man vanishing in the woods with the easy movements of a skilled woodsman that he realized that he didn't even know the name of this man to whom he had just told almost everything he knew.

Denny yawned. If it hadn't been for his worries about Bert and Bill and the menace of the gang of deer-jackers hanging over them, he would have wanted nothing better than to spend a few hours relaxing at the bearded man's camp. It was as pleasant a spot as he could wish— beside him the Yankee Kill tinkled and splashed, the hemlock branches chorused gently overhead, old Boot dozed by the little fire. Denny yawned again. He lay down, stretched out on the hemlock needle floor, and fell asleep.

Just what it was that awakened him Denny never knew. It was a loud and sharp sound—he was sure of that. It might have been a branch falling from a tree. A rock undermined by last spring's flood might have tumbled down the steep bank into the Yankee Kill. Denny knew that the woods often echo with startling sounds. Once he had seen and heard a great tree come crashing to the ground on a sunny and windless day. It looked strong, yet it was old and its time had come.

Denny struggled to his feet and looked around him. Boot, too, was on his feet, sniffing the air and giving an uneasy squeal from time to time. Could the sound that awakened him have been a shot? The hideout was not far away after all. Was it possible that whoever was in it had discovered Bert and fired at him? Once that thought came into Denny's head he couldn't remain idle. He had to go to the hideout and make sure Bert was safe. Luckily Boot was there; he would guard the man's camp in Denny's absence. And that leg was much better. Maybe because of the pill he'd taken or because he hadn't been hurt very much after all, he now could get around.

Denny pulled ashes over the fire and began hobbling away from the camp. Boot was tired after his day of exertion—he made only a token protest. Once across the Yankee Kill, Denny realized that he had done nothing to let the bearded man know where he was going. He pulled down the top of a red maple sapling on the bank and peeled the bark from a few feet of it. Then he bent the top in the direction of the hideout. The bearded man would be smart enough to get the meaning of a sign like that.

Five minutes of clambering through a stretch of boulder-strewn woods brought Denny to a huge oak tree. Such a tree was unusual in Yankee Hollow, which was too cool and moist for the taste of oaks. This tree had escaped the axes of generations of lumbermen because it branched out six feet from the ground—there wasn't a single good saw-log in the tree. Beneath the tree two plump grouse walked away as Denny approached. That was funny—the grouse didn't whirr upward as usual. Denny looked on the ground and saw why. Acorns lay everywhere. Denny knew that grouse find acorns too tough to open without help. But when an oak tree overhangs a road and the tires of passing cars crush the acorns, then grouse are likely to gather and eat themselves silly. Right at Denny's feet were tire marks and crushed acorns. He had found the old wood road that led up Yankee Hollow to the hideout. All he had to do now was to follow the tracks. For a few minutes everything went smoothly.

From somewhere up ahead came a crisp metallic clank. Denny thought he could make out a faint hum of human voices. The hum died away and Denny moved on. The unmistakable sound of a car starting up brought him to a halt. If there was a car at the hideout and it was going any place at all, it would have to go right over the spot he was standing on—and from the rattling and clanking that came to his ears it would get there quickly. Denny took to the woods and flattened himself behind a fallen tree. Very cautiously he raised his head in time to see a swaying and churning of branches up the road. *Bump-bang-clunk*—a jeep truck lurched into sight. Its green panel body was heavily scratched from pushing through the woods. A name had been painted on its side.

Where the driver's profile should have showed, there was a crazy-looking jumble—maybe the driver had a coat hung up beside him and that was what gave him a kind of nightmarish look as the coat flapped back and forth. In spite of the roughness of the road the truck was moving too fast for Denny to get a second look at the driver. But there was the license plate, nearly hidden from view by the deep nettles and ferns. That was a clue Denny had to see. He ignored the stab that shot down his leg as he got to his feet and crawled over the dead tree. But he was too late. A long-legged clump of laurel pushed aside by the truck snapped into place as the truck groaned past and hid all but the first letter—C. The truck gave a metallic rattle and vanished into the woods.

Denny clumped on toward the hideout. He hardly saw

where he was going because he was concentrating on something. Not long ago he'd seen a jeep truck like the one that had just passed, and it had had a name on its side. Could it have been the same truck? Denny felt sure that it was. Inside his head he tried to reach for the name. It had been a funny name: the first word was very short and it was divided in the middle. The last word was "Produce"—no, it was "Products." But that first word—it seemed to be on the point of jumping out of its hiding place in Denny's brain and then it jumped back in again.

A deerfly zoomed down on Denny and circled his head, buzzing loudly. Denny broke off a hemlock branch and chased the fly away. As he did that the word which had been playing hide-and-seek with him came out into the open—"X-L"—that was it, "X-L Wood Products." Denny had seen that truck a week before. It was going down the Meech Hollow Road one day at sunset. Well, maybe he had managed to grab a good clue at last.

The beech tree at the base of the hideout cliff had nothing hanging on it but leaves and a few nuts. The deer carcasses were gone, but Denny had expected that. The deer were in that truck, bouncing their way down Yankee Hollow to whatever market they were destined for. There was no sign of Bert on the ledge from which he was to watch. Denny stared at it for a long time.

When he saw a hawk swoop low over it a chill went down his back, for that might mean Bert wasn't there. A hawk isn't likely to glide that close to a human.

Where could Bert be? It wouldn't do to shout, for the deer-jackers might be nearby—or at least some of them. Yet all around it was as silent as the woods can get. It was the kind of thick silence that comes to the woods in early afternoon in late summer and early fall. Even the squirrels were taking it easy. The thought popped into Denny's head that Bert might have shifted his observation post and that now he couldn't keep an eye on the beech-tree clearing. If he climbed up to the hideout Bert couldn't miss him—unless . . . Well, it was better not to think of that.

It wasn't easy climbing up the cliff to the hideout. Denny's leg hurt. Probably the effect of that pill the bearded man had given him was wearing off. From time to time Denny rested, and each time the silence got more and more on his nerves. By the time he pulled himself up to the flat ledge in front of the door to the hideout he was ready to admit he was jittery.

The silence was just as deep in front of that sinister-looking door with its crisscrossing of barbed wire to keep porcupines from gnawing their way inside. There was no cry from Bert on the ledge above and no flash of his red cap. Then from somewhere behind the hideout door a faint scraping sound broke the silence that hung over the woods. It was followed by a *bang-bang-bang—*

bang. Something sounded as if it was rattling and sliding. A thing hit Denny's shoulder, fell to the rocky floor on which he stood, and noisily bounced down the cliff. It was a small piece of rock.

Denny stared upward. He saw a long brown object emerging from a hole in the mass of rock above the door. Was it the barrel of a rifle? In a flash Denny pressed himself as close as he could get to that barbed-wire door. The object above waggled as if it couldn't make up its mind. It paused as though baffled. Denny recognized it as being only a stick. The stick retreated inside the rocks. A hand emerged and carefully felt the outside of the rocks. It took a grip on a piece that stuck out and pulled it loose. A hail of rock bits hit the ledge behind Denny.

"Bert!" Denny shouted. That hand and that checked shirt cuff—they couldn't belong to anyone but Bert.

The hand and stick were hastily withdrawn. A muffled shout came from inside the hideout. Something slid and grated. Then *bang-bang-bang*—Bert was beating on the inside of the door. "Denny, is that you? Let me out of here, will you? I'm locked in. I can't get out!"

A loop of barbed wire with the barbs flattened out formed a kind of handle on the door. Denny pulled with all his might. Bert pushed. The door held as firm as the cliffs on Sawtooth Mountain. "I'll go crazy in here," came Bert's voice. "Denny, can't you get the door open?"

"I'm trying," Denny said. He yanked at the loop of

wire. It came away from the door. "We've got to figure this thing out, Bert."

"There are bars and things inside. That's what's holding the door," Bert shouted. "Come on, Denny, can't you get the door open?"

"How did you get locked in there?" Denny asked, then added, "I'm trying to find a way of breaking the door open."

Bert groaned. "I got to the observation place easily enough," he said. "And then I saw that if I wriggled along the cliff I could get to a much better place almost above the door to the hideout, with a thick balsam tree to hide behind. I heard talking inside the hideout. People seemed to be arguing, but I couldn't get a word. In a little while three men came out and went down the cliff. Look, Denny, why don't you get a rock and smash the door? I've got to get out of here."

"There isn't a loose rock that's big enough. I'm trying to get a thin one to pry the door open with. I think this one will do. If you saw those men you'd recognize them, wouldn't you?" Bert didn't answer. He started pounding and pushing from inside. From far away Denny heard a familiar sound: *Arh-arh-arh!* Boot was barking at the camp. Had the bearded man returned with help so quickly? No, that wasn't likely. Besides, Boot's barking sounded angry. A stranger must have approached the camp. The barking went on.

Denny told Bert about the camp and the bearded man.

Bert had stopped pounding. "It's no use," he muttered wearily.

"What happened after the men left?" Denny asked. He wanted to know, but more important than that, it would be good for Bert to have something to do while he waited for the door to be pried open. The first rock Denny had tried broke. He found another.

"I waited quietly until I heard a car start up and go away. Then I peeped out from behind the balsam and I saw that the door was wide open. I dropped down and went inside. But almost right away I knew I'd made a bad move. I heard the car coming back and in a few minutes somebody was coming up the cliff. I could hear him cursing somebody who must have been waiting down below. Then the shadow of a man passed across the floor of the hideout.

"I ducked behind a projecting rock in here. I heard a voice not six feet from me saying, 'Sure, you left it open, you fool! I tell you that door's got to be kept locked every minute! If it isn't we might all end up behind bars!' The door swung shut and the hideout went black. I heard a rattling and clicking as the door was locked.

"I held my breath until the sound of the car down below had faded away and then I tried the door and discovered that I couldn't open it. I didn't have my flashlight—it was in the pack I left behind that balsam. I saw a little light above the door and I tried to enlarge the hole it was coming through, but that was slow work. I had half a dozen matches and I used up all but one in trying to figure out a way of shoving back these iron bars that hold the door shut. I used my last match in rummaging around the place to try to find more matches. I didn't find any, but I did find a little blue composition book the deer-jackers must have used to keep track of the deer meat they sold. Here, I'll shove it under the door—I think the crack at the bottom will take it."

Denny didn't get what Bert was doing because Bert's voice was muffled as he bent down to push the book under the door. That was why the fresh breeze that hit at that moment beat Denny to the book. As he reached for it the book rustled across the ledge, opened up, and then rose like a bird. Helplessly Denny watched the book flutter and hesitate and finally come to rest on a dead branch high in a hemlock tree far below. It was plainly visible from where Denny stood.

Somehow the way that book acted struck Denny funny and he laughed as he told Bert where it had gone. It didn't seem a bit funny to Bert.

"What's the matter with you?" he cried out. "Here you fool around with the door and laugh when a valuable clue gets lost. Can't you understand that I'm not having any fun here in the dark. Maybe it's funny to you . . ."

Denny sobered up very quickly. "I'm doing my best

to get you out," he said. "The trouble is that I don't have any tools. I'm not getting very far trying to pry the door open with a rock. Here, I'll hand you my flashlight through that hole over the door and then maybe you can open the door from the inside. I should have thought of that before."

With the flashlight to help, Bert soon had the intricate system of bars inside yielding. But when the last one had been pushed back, the door still refused to open. Bert and Denny put all the pressure they could on the door, but it wouldn't stir. It was Bert who found the answer—there was a heavy lock embedded in the door. And of course neither of the boys had the key.

It wasn't until they had reached this stalemate that Denny realized that the steady barking of his dog had ended. From far down the Hollow a burst of wind carried a sound that might or might not have been made by Uncle Frank's jeep speeding along. Was it coming toward the hideout? Again Boot barked briefly. Without warning a stiff breeze roared mildly but steadily on the mountain above and drowned out all other sounds.

Five minutes went by. Then, twenty, thirty. An hour. The two boys pulled and tinkered and pushed at the door in vain. Bert announced that the flashlight was weakening. He went back to trying to enlarge the hole above the door with what little help Denny could give from a precarious perch on top of the door frame. The opening was far too small for even slim Bert to squeeze through.

By the time Bert had given up trying to get through the hole the sun was retreating and all the hideout except for a few trees on top was in shadow.

Once more Boot's barking soared up from the camp below. Denny came to a decision. "Bert," he said, "I'm going back to the camp to speed things up. Maybe they can't find the hideout. I'll follow the road back and maybe I'll meet the bearded man. If I don't, I'll be right back with plenty of matches and another flashlight. And I'll bring up a hatchet to knock the door open with."

An unhappy wail came from Bert behind the door. "It's terrible being locked up here, locked up in this thing. I don't know how much more I can take."

Denny hesitated. But he knew that every moment he stayed at the hideout added to the time Bert would have to stay inside. "I *have* to go and get something to open the door with. There's no other way. I'll hurry. I'll be just as fast as I can."

Down the cliff Denny went. Bert's voice followed him halfway down. "Hurry, hurry. . . . Hurry. . . ."

It was awkward and painful work getting down the cliff, and Denny was relieved when he had made it safely. The hike to the bearded man's camp went smoothly. It was all downhill and Denny knew the way by now.

Boot rejoiced as Denny approached. As the camp

came in sight it was plain that the dog had had good reason for excitement a little earlier. Someone had managed to keep just out of range of Boot's teeth and thoroughly ransack the camp. The bearded man's pack had been roughly emptied; bags and boxes had been dumped —the ground was littered with everything from envelopes of dried soup to a snakebite kit. The bearded man's watch, under a blanket of pancake flour, was still ticking.

Nothing seemed to have been stolen. The men Bert had seen at the hideout must have been the ones who gave the camp a going-over. It was only natural to want to find out all they could about the man who was camping so close to their base of operations.

Denny dug into the mess on the ground to gather up the things he'd promised to take back to the hideout. While Denny was hunting for the hatchet, Boot burst into an excited barking spell. The cause of Boot's warning quickly rattled through the woods across the Kill. It was Uncle Frank's red jeep with Uncle Frank and the bearded man aboard.

As the two men crossed the Kill, Uncle Frank was waving his arms the way he did when he told how he'd shot that big bear on Simmons' Flat. That meant he liked the bearded man—he didn't tell that story to just anybody.

Everything was being taken care of, Uncle Frank said. A state trooper would be up in an hour or so. The bearded man (Uncle Frank called him Phil) would go to a spot near the hideout and wait for the trooper, who seemed to know just where the place was without being told—

Denny butted in to say that there wasn't anybody in the hideout except Bert. He explained about his trip to the hideout and Bert's situation. Uncle Frank reassured him that they'd get Bert out of there fast.

The bearded man watched Denny giving a pained grimace as he shifted his weight from his ailing leg. "You're not going to the hideout," he said. "Not with that leg of yours. Anyway, your father wants you to come right home—he told me so on the phone. Your uncle will drive you there while I wait at the hideout. Then he'll join me."

Denny nodded. It was good to know that two capable grownups were taking over and lifting the burden of responsibility from his shoulders. At times that afternoon Denny had felt like a boy dressed in a man's clothing. He had felt as if he were trying to do more than he was capable of. He'd been glad to do it; now he was glad to be able to be his age again.

"Your mom sent you a message when I phoned," said Uncle Frank. "I don't pretend to know what it means. It goes, 'Remember the nomadic Kurds.'"

Denny laughed as he and his uncle headed for the jeep. That was just like Mom, he thought. He glanced back. The bearded man wasn't bothering to pick up his scattered belongings. He was putting first things first. He was fastening his hatchet on his belt and starting off to rescue Bert. He would take care of things here in Yankee Hollow. Denny was sure of that.

As the jeep started for Meech Hollow, Uncle Frank got Denny confused. In answer to Denny's question about where Bill was, Uncle Frank said Bill was still there and he'd found the plant. Uncle Frank had a way of taking it for granted that people knew a lot more than they really did. A few weeks before, for instance, he'd told Denny that old Benson was at it again. Denny had never heard of Benson, so he had to ask a lot of questions before he learned what was going on with Benson. It turned out that he was an old man who was very good at catching trout with his bare hands—"guddling" he called it. But that was illegal. Yet every once in a while the old man couldn't resist the guddling impulse. He'd done it again, and the game protector had found out and warned him that even though he put the trout back in the water, he'd be in trouble if he didn't stop.

Bill was at a tiny dead-end settlement on the other side of Sawtooth Mountain, Uncle Frank finally explained. The place was called Garrett's. He was working for Phil Bird—that was the bearded man—and Bill had gone to Garrett's for him. He'd gone to locate a plant. No, it wasn't a plant like the one Denny's dad worked in; there wasn't anything like that in Garrett's—only tumbledown houses and barns. It was the kind of plant that grows out of the ground. This company of Phil's was after plants, though what they wanted with the plants he didn't know. Maybe they were really after uranium and they could tell where it was by the kind of plants growing above it. "That would make sense," said Uncle Frank.

That was as much as Denny learned by the time he reached home. When Mom saw how tired Denny was she didn't say a word about the nomadic Kurds. She just got a swell dinner ready and made it plain that as soon as Denny had eaten he'd have to get right in bed with a good dose of Grandma Meech's herb liniment rubbed on his leg.

In between bites of fried chicken Denny asked Mom what had been happening while he was gone. Mom said, "Nothing much." She'd taken that deer meat they'd found on the doorstep down to Jesse Ames. There was nobody there but a man painting the porch floor, and he said she was the third to come there with deer meat in the past two days. He said it looked as if there were deer-jackers all over the place. Later Mom met Mrs. Gill at the meat counter of the Sooperdooper Market and she said with meat so expensive people were being tempted by all those deer running around. Some people said even the hamburger you got at a place like the Sooperdooper Market had some deer meat mixed with it.

Mrs. Gill said it was getting so people were afraid to

be out after dark. Over at what they call the Swamp Church, the other side of Tarrantville, only two people besides the minister got to prayer meeting the other day, and one was old Tom Elvey who was so deaf he didn't know what was going on. It wasn't only the jackers who had people scared; it was all this talk about devils being loose in the Catskills, too.

Denny had hit the coconut custard pie by this time and it made him feel so good that he said the police were after the jackers and pretty soon they'd have them. Then he yawned and stretched.

Mom said it wasn't enough to get the jackers. There would have to be some way worked out to make it possible for more deer to be shot by law-abiding people. There were too many deer around. The temptation to break the law was bound to be too much for some.

Denny hardly got under the covers with the spicy smell of that liniment filling the room when he fell asleep. When he woke up it was still dark. Outside a loud *Arh-arh-arh* echoed against the mountain. Something that had happened before seemed to be happening all over again. But that was Boot's bark! And wasn't Boot on the other side of the mountain?

As fast as his stiffened leg would let him, Denny got up and tumbled downstairs and out into the still night. The moon had set, leaving a silvery glow in the sky above the mountain. Boot's barking tapered off. He got Denny's scent and raced to him. "Good old Boot," Denny whispered. "How did you get here?"

Boot answered in the only way he could, by stepping up the tempo of his tail-wagging and by licking Denny's hands. Denny tied Boot in the woodshed and went into the house. He was puzzled. How had Boot managed to get back to the Hollow from across the mountain? He found the answer in a moment or two inside the house.

As Denny stepped into the living room he heard something that didn't belong there. It was the steady in-and-out of someone breathing. Denny felt for the light switch and turned it on. As the light filled the room the sound of heavy breathing stopped and Bert sat up from the couch on which he'd been sleeping. His explanation made his presence and Boot's very simple. Uncle Frank had driven both of them home. Mom had made up a bed for Bert in the living room so that he wouldn't awaken Denny upstairs.

"What happened at the hideout?" Denny interrupted.

Bert lay down again, facing the wall. "Oh, nothing much," he said. "They got the door open and then we picked up Boot and came here."

"But what did that state trooper say?" Denny asked.

Bert was slow in answering. "Oh—he just looked around and said, 'Um-hum.' That's all. Lemme sleep, will you?"

As he went upstairs to bed Denny couldn't help feeling annoyed with Bert. Denny went downstairs again.

"Did you tell the trooper about that notebook hanging in the hemlock?" he asked as he stood beside Bert again.

"Sure," Bert growled sleepily.

"And what did he say?" Denny persisted.

"He said, 'Um-hum,' " was Bert's answer. "Now leave me alone, will you?"

"I just wanted to know," Denny said.

"Now you know—let me sleep," Bert muttered sharply.

"O.K., O.K.," said Denny. And he groped his way up the dark stairs toward the light that glimmered from his room.

6) Strangers at the Door

ON SUNDAY mornings Mom always fixed something special for breakfast. This time it was sausages. Denny knew that because the odor of the sausages sputtering in the pan floated up the stairs to the bed where he lay, still half asleep. He sat up as he realized that something else besides the smell of sausage was coming up the stairs. Mixed with the smell were some startling words: "Four men believed to be members of a well-organized gang of deer-jackers who have been terrorizing parts of the Catskills eluded an elaborate police net last night at Garrett's, an isolated mountain settlement. They may be hiding out in the mountains, police warned—"

The voice of Joe Woolsome on the radio changed abruptly into a raucous blare of popular music. Denny jumped out of bed and went downstairs. He held his pajama bottoms up with one hand to keep from tripping. Mom had gotten them a little big so that he could grow into them. He heard Mom exclaim sharply, "Hank, why did you turn off Joe Woolsome and get that awful music? You'll wake up Dad. Now I'll have to turn Joe on again."

By the time Danny reached the kitchen Joe was on again. But he was saying that Peach-Bleach sure does take care of washday blues. That meant the news broadcast was over. Denny blinked and looked around the kitchen. Mom was busy at the stove; Hank was crawling on the floor, playing that Scampy the cat was a tiger in a jungle, with the legs of the table for the trunks of palm trees.

"Mom, where's Bert?" Denny asked. He wanted to talk with Bert the worst way now that he'd heard that bit about the deer-jackers on the radio.

"Bert?" Mom asked in the absent-minded way parents have sometimes. "Oh he must be around somewhere. Maybe he's still asleep. Or maybe he's gone out in the woods the way he does lots of times before breakfast. How about getting after those nomadic Kurds, Denny? Isn't this your last day to work on that paper?"

Denny said O.K., he'd take care of the Kurds. He sat down to breakfast, wishing that nomadic Kurds had never been invented.

"You can't put it off any longer," Mom began. Then Denny was saved from a hard few minutes by the ring of the telephone. Mom turned off the gas and grabbed the phone. She held it with one hand and served Denny and Hank their breakfast with the other, all the time saying, "Oh" and "You don't say so" and "Not really" in a polite way.

"That was Frances Dish," Mom explained after she'd

hung up. "She wanted to know if there was going to be any church today. Somebody told her that on account of those devils that are supposed to be loose in the Catskills they'd canceled church services. She said if you asked her, that was just the time they ought to have services. When I told Frances there would be services as usual, she said plenty wouldn't come because they were afraid to go out even on a Sunday. She told me Joe Woolsome said last night that a woman at the end of the Bergen Road had nailed her doors and windows shut and wasn't coming out of her house until the devils were sent back wherever they came from. I didn't hear Joe say that. Did you, Denny?"

"Nope," Denny answered glumly. He was waiting for Mom to get back to the Kurds.

Mom sat down and got at her own breakfast. She told Denny that her grandpa said they used to believe that when people started quarrying stone for sidewalks in the Catskills, it let out the devils the Lord had shut up inside the mountains. "But Grandpa always said that the funny noises people claimed they heard coming from the mountains were just the quarrymen whooping it up when they got paid off on Saturday nights. Now these jackers are another story—they seem more real after what Joe Woolsome just said. But, Denny, the realest thing in your life right now is that paper about the Kurds."

"Aw, Mom," Denny protested, "maybe those deer-jackers who got away from the police are hiding out somewhere nearby, maybe—"

Mom was firm. "Denny, I saw how you limped a little when you came down the stairs. That leg of yours isn't right yet. It'll do you good to have a quiet day, buckling down to getting at those Kurds. Then you'll get it off your mind and maybe later on you can go out."

After breakfast Denny went to his room and tried to get his mind on the nomadic Kurds. Outside the sun shone softly. The crows cawed in the orchard, answering one another and flapping back and forth as if playing a game. Denny heard Dad getting up and going downstairs. Again he smelled sausages cooking—this time for Dad. He heard Dad asking where Bert was. And when Mom answered that she didn't know, Dad said wasn't that just like Bert, always running off into the woods or somewhere.

Denny brought his mind back to the Kurds. He thought of how the Kurds liked to dance in a circle, all holding hands, and how when they danced somebody said they moved like a field of wheat rippling in the wind.

"I heard Joe Woolsome a little while ago—" That was Dad talking to Mom downstairs. "I think maybe that raid last night will quiet things down. I don't think we'll hear much about deer-jacking—at least not for a while." Mom said she agreed. She said she felt much better about the whole thing now. Even though the jackers got away, she was sure they'd be discouraged.

Denny sharpened his pencil. It didn't need sharpening. He just felt like giving it a better point. He straightened out the papers on the table under the attic window. The papers didn't need straightening out, but he did it anyway. He gave a sigh and began writing. He wrote steadily for a whole page. Then he began to feel drowsy —those crows cawing in the orchard, the breeze moaning under the eaves of the house, seemed to be hypnotizing him. His pencil moved slowly as Denny started his second page. It moved more slowly. Denny yawned.

"Hi, Bert!" That was Dad calling out loudly and cheerfully. "Come on, sit down and have your breakfast, Bert."

"We've been wondering whatever happened to you—" That was Mom.

Denny stopped yawning. He felt suddenly wide-awake. He heard Dad asking questions. He heard Bert answering in his slow, quiet way: "I went down the road as far as the old Elliott place. On the way I saw a funny thing. At first I couldn't imagine what to make of it. I thought I was seeing things—I really did. Because there were jeep tracks on the old road and when the tracks came to the fence they seemed to go right through it as if it wasn't there—"

"Well now, Bert . . ." Dad's voice sounded amused as if he didn't believe a word of what Bert was saying. But Bert went on to explain.

"I stood there a minute and I felt kind of frightened. And then I took hold of the fence and in a minute I knew what the story was. The old rusty fence wire was tight enough. But the posts on each side of the road were rotted off at the base. If you pushed against the wire, the posts just bowed down. That's what the jeep did. It drove against the fence. The fence wire lay down on the ground. And when the jeep went on, the wire swung back again. That's all there was to it."

Denny blushed. He should have thought of that himself. So much had happened that he hadn't gotten around to going back to that fence and trying to puzzle out its odd behavior. He'd simply forgotten the whole thing. Furiously Denny dug into the nomadic Kurds. They didn't have any fences, they didn't know what fences were, probably. The cawing of the crows grew dim. The voices downstairs merged with the low moaning of the wind and the rustling of the leaves on the sugar maple outside the window.

By the time the clock struck twelve Denny's paper was written. It wasn't as good as it might have been, Denny knew, but at least it was finished.

The next week rolled by as weeks do with sun and rain, good things and bad all mixed together. On Monday Miss Harvey announced that she was going to give everybody an extra week to get their papers polished up and maybe rewritten. Denny's old enthusiasm about the

Kurds came back and he decided to rewrite his paper so that he wouldn't have to feel ashamed of it.

That week Joe Woolsome didn't say a word about either deer-jackers or devils. Instead he got going about how there ought to be a new bridge across the Hudson River. In Meech Hollow a soothing haze made the mountains around seem unreal. Time seemed to drag along slowly. By night not a single strange sound broke the chorus of insect chirps. No deer-running pack of dogs bayed in the woods. Boot quieted down, and Denny decided to release him from his nighttime imprisonment in the woodshed.

The lavender haze of that week seemed to have gotten into Bert, for he seldom spoke and seemed to be living in a kind of dream. Denny was sure there was something on Bert's mind. But when he tried to find out what it was, Bert only said, "I'm O.K." He didn't get mad, he just seemed to be pushing people away.

On Saturday morning a cool breeze blew in from the west. It bustled and creaked among the treetops. It lifted the haze from the mountains. It even made Denny and Bert feel energetic enough to get at picking the apples they'd promised to Aunt Jessie—a couple of bushels of red Hubbardstons from those two big old trees along the lane. There was a wonderfully spicy preserve Aunt Jessie made with those apples, and she'd promised the boys all they could eat that winter.

The apples on the two trees looked fine from the outside, but inside each one was a family of worms. It was only on the topmost branches that good apples could be found. Denny was working away in the swaying tree-top when he heard a steady roaring from behind the mountain. The roaring grew louder and a small private plane emerged, turned sharply, and ducked behind the mountain again. The roaring died away. As Denny and Bert neared the kitchen door with their baskets of apples a different kind of roaring came from the direction of the valley. A black convertible with a pale top appeared at the beginning of the road. It raced toward the house as if the outcome of the World Series depended on it.

Denny and Bert ducked into the house to alert Mom.

"All kinds of things are happening this morning," Mom said as she hastened toward the door which was resounding with a series of knocks. "Uncle Frank phoned and said two strangers had been around Yankee Hollow asking all kinds of funny questions. Dad went over to get Frank quieted down. I hope this is just a salesman, but that car looks too expensive for one of them."

As the door swung open it revealed two men with their car glittering behind them. Mom said afterward that you could see that everything about those men cost plenty. Both took off their brown hats, and the tall top-heavy-looking one spoke in a slow, pleasant voice.

"I'm Ed James of the New York *Flash*, ma'am," he said. "And my friend here—he's Joe Megoney and he's on the *Flash*, too. We're doing a story on the deer-jacking here in the Catskills. I hope you'll be kind enough to help us out—

"I'm sorry," Mom said very firmly, "but I can't answer any questions." She began closing the door.

A hurt and surprised look came over the tall man's face and over his companion's as well. The tall man flushed and then Denny noticed a funny thing. One of his ears got as red as the front of the Sooperdooper Market, but the other one stayed the color it was before. The tall man said he wouldn't dream of asking questions— reporters didn't do that anymore, it was old-fashioned. All he wanted was a little information so that his story would be straight.

"If the public won't cooperate, ma'am," said the short man named Megoney, "how can the papers get things right?" He rubbed his hands. A ring with a large red stone sparkled.

Mom hesitated. She looked back at Denny. By this time Bert had done his vanishing trick again. Denny didn't know what to say. "Well," he began, hoping the right words would come to him, "we really don't know anything except rumors and little bits—"

The tall man beamed at Denny. "Fine. That's the proper spirit. To evaluate the evidence—"

The short man clapped his hands. "Bravo," he muttered sourly. "Come on, Ed. Let's not get intellectual. We got to hurry."

The tall man stopped. He flushed. Again Denny saw one ear light up like the taillight of a car when you step on the brake. The other ear refused to go along.

Mom made it plain that she had made up her mind. "I'm sorry," she said, "but we really don't know enough to make it worthwhile talking about it."

Megoney stepped forward and thrust his bold, round face toward Mom and Denny. "What about that venison —that deer meat, I mean—you found on your porch?" he asked. "We know about that. Now, come on, lady. Let's get talking."

At that point Hank darted into the picture. He was wearing a copper pot on his head because he was being a knight in armor. He pointed at the porch floor. "It was right there," he announced. "We found it right there."

Megoney chuckled and backed away from the door. "See, lady? You know plenty. Let's hear about it."

The tall man stood in silence. The flush retreated from his face. Once more his ears became mates. "Ma'am," he began with a smile, "all we want are a few facts. In the public interest, ma'am, I assure you—"

Mom shook her head. "I'm sorry," she said as she closed the door.

Denny watched through the narrow hall window. The two men gave the door a final knocking while Mom walked back to the kitchen, and then Denny slipped the old-fashioned bolt across in case the men should try to open the door. He saw them give up and walk back toward their car. For a moment they disappeared behind the lilac bushes. Denny saw them reflected in the sleek side of their car. Their figures were grotesquely distorted. They looked as if they were underwater. Suddenly they reappeared. Both halted and stared upward.

Denny became aware then that the roar of a plane was making the air vibrate all around him—louder and louder, as if the house were its target. The men outside smiled and waved toward the sky. The roar receded. The men got in their car and sped away.

Denny asked Mom what she thought the two men wanted. "I can't imagine," Mom answered. "They didn't act like anyone I'd ever met before. All I'm sure of is that they were from New York City. Their car had a New York City license number—I got that much." Mom looked up from the dirty dishes that filled the kitchen sink. "It used to be there was a big difference between city people and country people. But there isn't so much anymore. Plenty of times you can't tell the two kinds apart. But there was something very different about those two—" Mom paused. "Somehow I felt I didn't understand them. I was even a little afraid."

Denny said he'd never seen any reporters, except of course for Joe Woolsome, and he looked exactly like anybody else only he was a little rounder. Maybe the two men *were* really reporters from a city paper. Maybe that plane they waved to had a photographer on board taking pictures for the New York *Flash*.

Mom said, "Maybe." Then she asked Denny to go call Boot. That half a sausage Hank had dropped was still under the table and Boot might as well pick it up. But Denny didn't call Boot for a while. As he opened the door Dad's jeep came roaring up the road. And when Dad stepped out he had a story to tell.

"I've never seen Uncle Frank more stirred up than he was a little while ago," Dad began. "Two men had just come to see him and they said they loved to hunt and fish and they were looking for a place to buy where they could put up a shack to use when they went hunting and fishing. But they didn't look as if they knew a trout from a raccoon and it didn't take long for Uncle Frank to find out that their looks weren't misleading. They were city people who were as ignorant of country things as it's possible to get."

"Did they have a big black convertible?" Denny asked eagerly.

Dad turned a startled look on Denny. "They sure did, but how did you know that?" he asked.

Mom and Denny, talking by turns, explained.

Dad shook his head. "Those fellows who came here and the ones who talked to Frank were the same pair all right. They told you they were reporters. They told Frank they were looking for land to buy. There's something very fishy about those two. Uncle Frank thought so. He told them he didn't want to sell any of his land. One of the men said he was sure Frank would change his mind because he had plenty of money—he could pay a good price."

"That's no way to talk to Uncle Frank," Mom exclaimed.

"You're right," Dad agreed. "After the men said that, Frank told them, 'Nobody in all the world has enough money to buy my land—if I don't want to sell it.' He asked them to clear out and stay cleared out. The men knew there was no use arguing. They cleared out fast."

"And then the men must have come right over here. No wonder they acted funny after the way Uncle Frank talked to them," Mom said, then asked Denny again to call Boot so that he could pick up that half a sausage before somebody stepped on it. As Denny stood at the door calling the dog he remembered that Boot hadn't been around for a while. He hadn't been there to bark when the two strangers came, he hadn't welcomed Dad with his usual excited jumping. Denny called the dog once more. There was no answer.

Mom said that come to think of it Bert had said something about Boot just before those two men knocked on the door. Maybe he knew where the dog was and had gone after him. She wasn't sure just what Bert had said —lately he sort of mumbled sometimes instead of speaking up.

A loud *clonk-clonk* interrupted Mom. Hank was coming down the stairs, dragging his wooden car after him and letting it give the loudest possible bump on each step. When the racket stopped Dad said he wished Bert had told somebody where he was going. It wasn't right for people to wander off without letting those who were responsible for them know where they'd gone. With Bert's parents away it was up to him to take care of Bert, Dad said. He'd give Bert a talking to.

Hank was standing at the foot of the stairs unwinding his car's towrope from around his legs. He looked up at Dad and said, "Gone to Slosson's." Mom questioned Hank, and soon it began to look as if Bert had really told Hank that he'd gone to Slosson's.

Denny knew Slosson's well enough. It was an abandoned farm across the high ridge to the northeast of Meech Hollow. There a man named Slosson had made a clearing in the forest more than a hundred years before. He'd built his house right at the bottom of a high cliff. It had been gone for years and now there was nothing left but a cellar hole and the remains of an apple orchard. All around the woods were coming back—there were big trees now where Slosson had once grown his hay and corn. People liked to camp there because a fine spring trickled out of the base of Slosson's Cliff and there were lots of raspberries and apples and things to eat.

Dad looked at his watch, "Let's take a look at Slosson's, Denny," he said. "We can be there and back in forty minutes."

Denny often thought that there must be some kind of law of nature that went to work the minute anybody was on the point of doing something he really wanted to do —like taking that walk to Slosson's. This time the law brought to the door old Harry Simmons, the town superintendent of highways. "Just taking a look around Meech Hollow," Harry boomed in that big voice of his. "Wanted to see if there was any work needed doing before the fall rains set in. Now that culvert by the old chestnut stump down the road—guess that ought to be replaced because it doesn't carry off the water the way it should." Then Harry got going about deer hunting, and that was only natural because he was one of the best hunters around—he always got his deer the first day of the deer season.

"Now about this here deer-jacking everybody's talking about," Harry began, "my old granddad jacked many a deer in his day, but then it was perfectly legal. Then, when deer commenced to get scarce, they passed a law forbidding jacking and then granddad didn't jack any more deer. I still have the lamp my granddad used when he jacked deer. It's a little tin thing with a reflector. You clipped it to the front of your cap and it burned kerosene oil. Someday I'll have it electrified and then I'll set it on the wall inside the front door. Real old relic, that lamp is."

"The people who jack deer these days don't use any old kerosene lamps," Dad remarked.

"Nosirree," said Harry, "those fellows use the most modern gadgets—they've brought deer-jacking up to date. Now I've been told, and I can't say by whom, that they sell their deer meat to fancy clubs and restaurants, so the meat has to be the very best quality. They don't want any meat from deer who've been loading up on acorns on the mountain because that makes the meat bitter. They want deer who've been hanging around old orchards—for instance, places like this here, or Yankee Hollow or over to Slosson's. And they dress the meat like a professional butcher—it's handled like the meat you buy in a store."

"Half the people who shoot deer spoil the meat by not dressing it right," said Dad.

"You can say that again," Harry said. Then he started telling Dad exactly how to handle a deer after it was shot. By this time Harry was sitting at the kitchen table having a cup of coffee with Dad. Denny had heard Harry tell the same story three or four times before, so he said he guessed he'd run over to Slosson's and see if Bert and Boot had gone there. Dad said he'd go too only he had to take Aunt Hattie to church in another ten minutes.

Denny said, "O.K." He waited a minute to listen to Harry saying that the old-timers always said that the way to get really tasty deer meat was to jack a deer. If you chased one forty miles around the mountains before getting a chance to shoot it, the meat wasn't worth eating. These big-time jackers seemed to know that. They were hand-in-glove with the gangsters who controlled so many big-city night clubs and gambling places—if they didn't supply good meat they'd be taken for a ride.

Harry was still talking away as Denny left and cut through the lot across the brook to get on the trail for Slosson's. The trail wound around the base of a high, steep ridge and led Denny higher and higher until it took him to the edge of the small plateau where Slosson had hacked out his little farm. Usually it was a peaceful-looking place, but this time it wasn't.

There were jeep tracks all over. Bushes and blackberry plants were pushed down. The remains of half a dozen deer had been tossed into Slosson's cellar hole. Some animal—probably Boot—had dragged out a deer head and chewed it up on the grass near the spring. From the looks of things it seemed clear that the jackers had been at work the night before. Probably Bert had gotten wind of it in that quick way of his and come here to check. Or maybe he'd followed Boot—Denny had slipped up on keeping the dog tied.

"Hey, Bert!" Denny shouted. "Boot! Come, Boot!" The only answer was a series of echoes from the high cliff behind the cellar hole. For a few minutes Denny did some thinking. He walked to the spring at the base of the cliff and lay down to lap up a drink. It was won-

derful water—the best this side of the mountain, Dad
often said. No wonder Slosson had settled beside the
spring more than a century ago even if most of his fields
were as tilted as the roof of a barn, and his cows had to
be half mountain goat to manage to graze on the steep
pastures on the mountain above. Now the spring was
being put to other uses. Campers used it in the summer
and perhaps last night the deer-jackers had washed up
beside it, for dressing deer can be a messy business. Yes,
there was a smear of dried blood on the flat stone beside
the spring. Denny kicked at a bit of white showing
among the maple leaves on the ground. Yes, it was a
bunched-up piece of paper toweling the jackers had
used.

Denny sat beside the spring and looked around him.
Long ago old Slosson had butchered his hogs and cut
up deer beside this very spring. Here he had skinned the
muskrats and mink he trapped, and maybe tanned the
skins of the bears he shot so that his children might use
them as blankets during the cold winters that buried his
little log cabin under drifts of snow. Slosson had been
more of a hunter and trapper than a farmer—plenty of
people in the mountains had earned their living that
way long ago. It was a perfectly good way to earn a
living, Denny thought. It wasn't a bit like the dishonest
way of the jackers who had used Slosson's spring the
night before.

A chipmunk chattered at Denny from a broad crack

that ran up the cliff above the spring. The chipmunk stared at Denny and set off a volley of exclamations before vanishing into his refuge inside the cliff. A tiny bit of stone set in motion by the chipmunk's feet struck the leaves beside Denny.

That crack that ran up the cliff—it was easier to climb along it than it looked and it led to a short cut to Meech Hollow. Slosson had used it, they said, when he went up the mountain to get his cows from the pasture. He'd used it when he wanted to get to a neighbor in a hurry. Denny had often climbed it, and once he'd helped a reluctant Boot up the crack.

Maybe that was what Bert had done. Maybe he had guessed that Boot had come to Slosson's to eat deer meat. Maybe he had found him and gone back to Meech Hollow by the short cut. That would explain why Denny hadn't met Bert at Slosson's or on the way over. Well, it would be easy to check that possibility. Denny sprang to his feet and stared up the crack.

Once you got going on the crack the way was easy. It was only the first five feet that were too narrow and steep to give a good foothold. It wasn't possible for an unaided dog, for example, to climb that first bit. But if you picked up the dog and held him high against the cliff, his front feet would take hold after a bit of scrambling. It was easy enough for a man or a boy to pull himself up, but a dog doesn't have any hands to grip the rocky projections with.

Yes, there was the place where Boot, only a little while before, had scratched loose some of the earth lodged in the crack and torn up a goldenrod plant trying desperately to make a living in a tiny pocket of soil. Boot and Bert had taken this route back to Meech Hollow—that seemed certain.

Denny tested his footing at the base of the crack, then climbed up the cliff and headed back home.

As he came to his house he wasn't at all surprised at seeing Boot frisking down the drive to meet him. He wasn't surprised either to see Bert sitting on the porch step looking gloomily over the orchard. Denny petted Boot and pulled at a few burs clinging to the dog's throat. He had seen the same kind of burs growing beside the spring at Slosson's.

"Hi, Bert," Denny sang out.

Bert was slow in answering. Finally he managed an unenthusiastic "Hi!"

"I guess you and Boot were at Slosson's," Denny said. He felt a little proud of having figured that out. Bert only nodded in a vague way and continued to stare across the orchard.

"I guess you saw that the deer-jackers had been at Slosson's," Denny said.

"Sure," was Bert's answer.

"Did you follow Boot to Slosson's?" Denny asked.

"Um," Bert replied.

"Look here, Bert, what's the matter with you anyway?" Denny asked the question more sharply than he'd intended.

"Nothing. I'm O.K.," Bert answered. He got up and went inside the house. Denny listened to Bert tramping upstairs. Then he came to a decision and followed Bert on up.

7) *A Flood and a Rescue*

BERT WAS sitting on his bed frowning at his open arithmetic book. Denny dug out his paper on the nomadic Kurds and frowned at that. He sat on the edge of his bed and frowned some more. This was his last chance to do a good job on that paper, and he didn't feel a bit like tangling with the nomadic Kurds. Not with Bert sitting eight feet away with half the gloom in the world spread over his face. Denny cleared his throat.

"Bert," he began, "what's the matter? You act so unhappy lately." That was the wrong thing to say.

"Oh, leave me alone," Bert growled savagely. He frowned at his book more fiercely than ever. Denny saw his lower lip jutting out and his eyes blinking as if tears were close to appearing. For a moment Denny frowned at his Kurds. He glanced up and met Bert's miserable-looking eyes.

"Why are you staring at me?" Bert shouted.

"I wasn't staring," Danny protested.

"You were so," Bert insisted.

Denny glanced through the window at the sunny world

outside. No doubt about it, something was on Bert's mind. Something that upset him dreadfully. But what could it be?

Denny turned to Bert and spoke softly. "Bert, ever since that time we were in Bill's hideout, you've been different. Something must have happened to bother you—"

With a bang that made Denny jump, Bert slammed his book shut. "How can I study if you won't leave me alone?" he demanded. "I've got work to do—can't you see that?"

Denny got up and strode toward the door. He turned toward Bert and said very quietly, "All right, then, if you want to keep it to yourself and go on feeling miserable—O.K. All I want to do is to help you. If you tell what's on your mind to somebody, then you'll feel better. I gave you the chance. If you don't want to take it, that's your business." Denny started out the door. But he stopped when he heard a single pleading sound from Bert.

"Denny—" Bert called out. In a moment Denny was sitting beside Bert. "All right," Bert said, "I'll tell you. I know I should and at the same time I don't want to. I've been all pulled apart lately."

"It started that day we went to the hideout, didn't it?" Denny asked.

Bert nodded. "After you left me there to go to get

help, I was frightened. I lay down on the floor of the
hideout and closed my eyes. It was warm and stuffy in
there, maybe that's why I fell asleep. When I woke up in
a little while I saw a weird greenish light flickering on
the ceiling. I jumped up and saw something that made
my flesh creep." Bert stopped and seemed to be pulling
himself together before he went on.

"At the end of the hideout I saw two—well—two
things standing with that greenish light glowing on their
faces. I thought of witch doctors in the jungle. That's
what they reminded me of. They had crazy half-animal
faces and they just waited there with that awful light on
them. I gave a yell and then they vanished and it was
black dark all around. Denny, was I seeing things?
Things that weren't there? Am I going nuts?"

Denny laughed. "Of course, you're not," he said.
"You've got the sharpest eyes and the most sensible head
of anybody I know. If you saw those things they were
there all right."

Bert shook his head. "I don't know," he said, "I tell
you I shiver every time I think of the things, and every
time I wonder if I really saw them. I was all alone in
there and the door was locked. How could anything
get in?"

"I'll bet they got in somehow," Denny said. "How
about taking a look at the hideout next Saturday?"

"I wouldn't go there alone for anything, but I'll go

with you." Bert smiled for the first time in days. "It's a deal for Saturday. Maybe we'll find out then that there really are devils loose in the Catskills."

"If we find any, we'll take them to Joe Woolsome—how about it?"

"O.K.," Bert agreed cheerfully.

Monday, Tuesday, Wednesday—the days of that week crawled by, one by one. Denny handed in the paper about the Kurds which he had rewritten Sunday night. Bert failed an arithmetic test. The sun shone every day and old people said so fine a spell of September weather meant a hard, cold winter was on its way. Just as Denny had decided that Saturday would never come, there it was in its usual place. And there he and Bert were stalking upward from the house with the mournful cries of poor chained-up Boot following them and slowly melting away.

The sun which had shone so pleasantly all week on the roof of the Mountain Central School now chose this day of freedom to duck behind a cloud. There was a bite in the wind as the boys started out. By the time they were halfway up Meech Mountain they had entered a cloud which was rudely ignoring the weather report's prediction of a fair day. The mountaintop was a foggy wasteland from which familiar landmarks had vanished. The boys missed the turn for Beech Ridge and had to backtrack to find it.

No sooner were the two safely on Beech Ridge than a

gentle rain began to fall and little puffs of wind shook moisture from the treetops with the effect of a traveling showerbath. The air grew chilly.

"Let's get there the quickest way—that's to the top of Sawtooth and then down to the hideout with a rope. This weather is terrible. Gosh—I'm cold."

After that neither Denny nor Bert made any attempt to keep dry. They let every bush they met discharge its load of water on them. They stepped boldly in the puddles which had formed in every depression in the rocks. The gentle rain turned into a violent and windy downpour by the time the boys reached the gnarled spruce tree which stood on the cliff above the hideout. The storm was roaring and groaning at the top of its voice. Denny peered over the edge of the cliff at the muddle of rocks and branches that marked the roof of the hideout. No smoke rose from the chimney—the place looked deserted.

"O.K., let's go," Denny called out in an effort to shout down the wind. Bert looped his rope around the trunk of the spruce tree and sent its ends dangling against the hideout's door. Denny slid down. Bert followed. There was no need to use the short iron bar with which Denny had weighed down his pack, for the door was unlocked. It swung open at a touch.

"It's too good to be true," Bert muttered. He and Denny stood for a moment in the stream of warm and musty air coming from inside the hideout. "Hello!

Hello!" Denny shouted. There was no answer. The boys gingerly stepped inside and out of the driving rain. A hasty examination of the place brought the good news that it was indeed empty and that no one was lurking in a dark corner waiting to tackle them. The scanty supply of firewood in the woodbox was quickly crackling in the stove and the oil lamp they found in a corner was lighted. Wet clothing and boots began drying on a line above the stove, and the boys were doing their best to fill some old shirts and pants of Bill's which they found in the hideout.

Denny's pack hadn't been up to keeping out the rain that morning, so the lunch Mom had packed turned out to be mushy except for the oranges. A hasty rummaging in the hideout produced a can of ravioli and another of baked beans. Both were quickly opened and their contents set to bubbling on the stove.

As the boys were eating, a sound at the back of the hideout brought them to their feet. With the help of their flashlights they hunted for the source of the sound. "Look, Bert!" Denny called out. A trickle of water was entering the hideout from the base of the back wall. It was moving across the floor in the direction of the door.

"That noise we heard—it must have been some rocks moving back there under the pressure of the water. They shifted and now the water is getting in. That's one thing Bill was worried about when he fixed up this place. He thought it might not be too dry in a heavy storm because it seems to be right in the path of a channel that carries water off the mountain."

There was no stopping the stream of water. It grew increasingly vigorous. Bert took Denny's iron bar and made a little ditch to guide the water along one wall and out under the door. By that time the ceiling had begun to drip in a dozen places. An occasional drop of water hit the hot stove and hissed sharply.

Outside the roaring of the storm grew louder. Denny and Bert looked at each other uneasily. "It's getting worse. We may have to stay here all night," Denny said.

"Well, we might be in worse places," Bert answered. As he spoke a loud crash made the very rocks seem to shake. The door was flung wide open and a leafy branch was thrust inside.

Denny and Bert ran to the door. "There's been a little slide up above," Bert yelled, "and this birch tree has come down. Let's haul it in. We may need the wood for the fire before the night is over."

Getting the tree inside proved to be harder than it seemed at first. Its mass of roots was uncooperative and had to be hacked short before it would enter through the door. When the tree was at last inside, the boys were wet and muddied from head to foot. Outside the rocks and earth which had slid down with the tree were waiting to be cleared away. And that had to be done fast. Already the outlet of the stream that ran across the floor was choked by the debris outside. The stream was rapidly widening until it threatened to cover the entire floor.

It was half an hour before Denny and Bert could sit down by the stove again and finish their lunch. By then the wind and rain outside had slowed down a little. But the drip from the ceiling was wetting everything and the stream still gurgled across the floor.

Every now and then the boys jumped up and shoved things from under a drip or raised them out of the water on the floor. They kept an eye on a couple of cartons full of blankets—it might be tough if those got wet. After a while a *pit-pit-pit* sent Denny racing to the back of the cave. The ceiling was dripping in a new place and water was drumming on one of the cartons. But that wasn't all. A trickle of water sneaking in through the wall had dissolved the glue in the bottom of one. When Denny lifted it the bottom opened up and everything inside spilled on the floor. Part of the stuff tumbled into the stream that was running across the floor.

Denny turned the beam of his flashlight on some things that had begun floating with the current. "Look, Bert," he shouted, "those must be the faces you saw here that last time! They're nothing but masks!"

The masks swayed this way and that in a sort of eerie dance. They looked almost alive until the current had taken them as far as it could. Piled up against the bottom of the door, they seemed to die and become mere masks again.

Bert grabbed one of the things and held it up. "This is

one of the faces I saw," he said. "It's got the same sort of fur beard and the same little horns on its forehead. Gosh —it's a crazy thing. No wonder I was scared."

Denny was down on his knees looking over the other masks. "One of these wouldn't have been a bad thing to have had when we were out in the rain," he said. "They're made of plastics and things—they ought to be waterproof." He shook the water from a brown-and-white mask with a black lumpy nose. He slipped it over his head. He took it off when he noticed how tense Bert looked when he saw it.

"I didn't see just those two masks," Bert protested. "There were two people wearing them. They couldn't have gotten in through the door because it was locked, and anybody unlocking it would have awakened me. There must be a secret entrance to this cave."

Before long the two boys had given the place a thorough going-over, but they hadn't found an opening big enough to let in a cat. They went at it again. The floor, the ceiling, every crack and dark recess was looked at and felt and pushed and pried at. The boys sat down on the log that did duty as a bench beside the stove and admitted that they had done their best and had failed to locate the secret entrance. But Bert was cheerful anyway. Seeing the masks had taken a big weight from his mind—he knew at last just what it was that had frightened him so badly, even though he didn't know the whole story.

Bert jumped up. "Come on, Denny, let's get going," he said. "We found out what we wanted to find out here —part of it anyway. Now let's try to get home again. It sounds as if the storm is about over." Bert threw the door open and he and Denny stepped outside.

The rain had stopped and the clouds were hastily retreating. Here and there a patch of blue was showing. But there was still water everywhere. A thin waterfall splashed down the cliff above and hit the ledge on which the boys stood. A mighty roaring from below told how the Yankee Kill had overflowed its banks when the rainfall became too much for it to handle. Through breaks in the treetops below water could be seen foaming and gurgling among the trees and rocks and even invading the clearing below where the boys had seen those deer carcasses hanging from the big beech tree.

"Look!" Bert whispered. He pointed past the beech tree at an unexpected sight. The jeep truck which Denny had last seen working its way down Yankee Hollow past the doctor's camp was now deep in swirling water twenty feet from the big tree. As Denny looked he saw something moving behind the windshield. The truck wasn't empty—there seemed to be two men inside. The boys ducked but they were too late. A muffled and anguished voice rose from below. Denny cautiously peeped over the edge of the rocky platform and saw a familiar face. It was that of the man who called himself Ed James.

James was leaning out the half-open door of the truck.

The man was shouting and occasionally helping himself along with a wave of an arm. But for all Denny or Bert could get, he might have been shouting in Kurdish. One phrase got through the mighty roaring of the water —"We're freezing in here." Then the man seemed to go back to Kurdish again. But by that time he had made it clear that he wanted help in getting out of the truck. He and his pal were marooned by the flood. Denny gave Bert a questioning look. "Maybe part of the gang of deer-jackers is in that truck," he said. "But if they need help—"

"O.K.," Bert said slowly, "I guess we'll have to try to help them. Maybe they really are reporters. We don't know yet who they are."

"Probably they've been stuck all the time we were at the hideout. I never looked down."

"I didn't either," Bert said. He grabbed the rope which still hung down the cliff from the big spruce tree and pulled it down. "Denny, get my hatchet out of the hideout and then let's go."

The slide down the cliff was wet and muddy. The foot of water into which the boys splashed at the bottom was chilling. But the encouraging shouts of the men in the truck spurred them on over projecting rocks and stumps to within ten feet of the truck.

"Hey!" shouted the man they recognized as Ed James.

"Come on—" shouted the short man, Joe Megoney.

"What happened?" Denny shouted above the gurgling and splashing of the water.

"We got stuck," explained Ed James. "The water killed the motor. We've been stuck here for hours. We're c-c-c-c-cold. Get us out of here fast. Be a good neighbor and get us out of here."

"B-b-b-be a g-g-good neighbor," chimed in Megoney. "We tried to get out but we g-g-got wet. We're freezing. Yeah, be a good neighbor, fellows."

"What are you doing here in Yankee Hollow?" Denny shouted.

Ed James said, "Whassat? Hey? Can't understand."

"C-c-c-can't understand," echoed Megoney. "Come on, be a good neighbor and get us out of this thing."

Bert tossed one end of his rope to Megoney. "Here. Tie your end to the steering post and we'll hold this end. The water's running pretty fast, but it's only up to your knees. Hang on to the rope and you'll be all right."

The men on board the truck talked it over. In a bungling way Megoney tried to tie the rope to the steering post. Ed James elbowed him aside and tied it all over again. Then the two men talked. Megoney seemed to be making objections.

"My friend says he won't step in that water for anything," James called out. "He's got to have something to walk on—like a bridge made out of something—"

"Sure we could make a bridge by chopping down some

trees. But with only one hatchet it would take time—"

"Do it then. We're frozen to death already. What does it matter if we get frozen some more? But hurry."

"Get us out fast. I've never been so cold in my l-l-l-life," Megoney wailed. His blue lips and chattering teeth showed he wasn't fooling. He banged the door of the truck shut. He and his companion huddled inside without speaking or moving.

Ten feet isn't much of a distance to someone who's running or riding in a car. But when that ten feet is the length of a bridge made with a single hatchet across a swiftly running stream of water, it can seem like a mile. It took half an hour for Denny and Bert to cut the first of the birch logs with which they intended to make the bridge. Then Denny slipped and the log was whirled away by the water. An hour later the bridge was finished and the two bedraggled men in their wet and rumpled city clothes were gingerly crossing it with the help of a rope to which they clung anxiously. Ten minutes of pulling, pushing, and encouraging words by the boys got them to the safety of the hideout.

A roaring fire in the stove plus a pot of tea quickly got the rescued men thawed out. And as they warmed up they began asking questions. What were the boys doing at the hideout? Had they ever been there before? Bert left the answering to Denny. Denny's attempts at being evasive only seemed to bring the two men to a kind of boiling point. Megoney stamped his foot on the floor and said that if the boys didn't give him straight answers they'd be sorry.

"Take it easy, Megoney," James interrupted. "Give the boys a chance to talk before you start threatening them."

Megoney glared at Denny. He shook a fist at him. "Come on, now, start talking," he screamed.

The tall man moved toward Bert as if to keep him from interfering in whatever he expected to happen.

"Look here—" Bert began.

"Shut up," the little man shouted. "Your turn will come later."

Denny felt anger building up inside him. He and Bert had a perfect right to be in the hideout—it belonged to their cousin Bill. They had gone to a lot of trouble to rescue these two men and they hadn't even said "Thank you."

Megoney glared at Denny. "Come on now—talk," he snarled.

Denny stared back in silence. He wouldn't talk. He wouldn't say a word. Whatever Megoney might do he would never drag a single syllable from his lips.

Megoney's stare faltered. He glanced at James standing beside Bert, some six feet behind Denny. "You're the brains of this operation," he said, "you say what we do next."

James moved away from Bert. He stepped close to Megoney and began whispering in his ear. Megoney

smiled. He took his eyes off Denny and whispered something in his friend's ear.

Denny saw his chance and took it. A long tough branch of the birch tree which had crashed inside the door earlier was lying on the floor. Megoney stepped over it in order to reach James's ear. With all the speed he could develop, Denny seized the end of the branch nearest him and gave it a yank to one side. Megoney's legs buckled. He toppled over and splashed into the stream still running across the floor. James stood still as a statue for a second, then he stepped toward Megoney. By that time Denny had reached the door. Bert was a few steps ahead and already outside.

Over the ledge they went with shouts and curses ringing behind them. As they slid down the treacherous trail a shower of rocks whizzed by without touching either of them. They reached the bottom in safety and in time to hear Megoney's voice from above saying that it was all a mistake—he had just been kidding. The tall man's high-pitched laugh followed. "We were just kidding," he shouted.

"Let's make for Uncle Frank's," Bert whispered. "We can go along the side of the mountain and keep above the water in the valley. If we try to go to your house we'll never make it before dark, and our flashlight and packs and everything are still there in the hideout."

Every trace of the storm of that afternoon had vanished from the sky. Already the sun was low enough to set a cloud aglowing with orange fire. There was a chill in the air that made Denny shiver. He realized then that he'd left his jacket behind in the hideout. "Let's hurry, Bert," he suggested. "We'll have to run if we want to keep warm."

"I'll do my best," Bert answered soberly. And it was only then that Denny realized his cousin had left his soaked boots drying beside the stove. He was now barefooted and there were several miles of rough going ahead of him. Denny came to an abrupt stop. "Bert, we've got to do something. You can't go on barefooted —not over this rough country."

"Well, I've got to," Bert answered. "Come on, Denny, every minute counts."

Suddenly Denny took off one boot and handed it to his cousin. "Here," he said." Luckily my feet are only a little bigger than yours. We'll each wear one boot—that ought to help a lot."

It did help as the two went on. But not for long. A rough rock bruised Bert's bare foot and Denny stubbed his toe painfully. But at least they were at a safe distance from the hideout, and they could take a few minutes to stop and think without expecting to hear Megoney and James come blundering along in pursuit.

Luckily Bert had his jackknife in his pocket. He got to work cutting bark from a yellow birch tree growing against the rock on which they were sitting. They set off again with rough bark moccasins fastened to their unshod feet with handkerchiefs and bits cut from Denny's bootlaces. They clumped along awkwardly enough and with a pause now and then to get stones and pieces of wood out of their bark moccasins. Soon it became possible to take to the valley and follow the wood road that led from the hideout.

The light began fading from the sky and a strong breeze rustled its way down the Hollow. The boys groped their way along as the first star peeped through the swaying branches overhead. At last the road led them out of the woods and over a gate into Uncle Frank's pasture. Ahead a faint but warm sparkle of light appeared—it came from Uncle Frank's house. Denny managed to break into a clumsy run.

"Come on, Bert," he called, "we're almost there."

Bert hung back. "Ouch," he said, "I've got blisters from that boot of yours. It's all I can do to walk."

"Sorry," said Denny. He and Bert clumped along toward the light. Uncle Frank's four rangy hounds got their scent and bounded to them barking with all their might. The door of the house opened and Uncle Frank stepped out and called the dogs. To the boys coming out of the darkness his voice sounded like music.

As they poured out their story Uncle Frank's face grew serious. "I don't like it," he said. "I don't like having those two men up there—"

"Let's call the state troopers," Denny said, moving toward the phone on the kitchen table.

Uncle Frank laughed. Aunt Jessie turned toward Denny as she took the roast lamb out of the oven. "Why, Denny, don't you know?" she said. "The storm knocked out the telephone and it flooded the road down below. Those men up there and all of us are stuck in Yankee Hollow till tomorrow morning at least."

"Stuck?" roared Uncle Frank. "Not with those fellows cornered up there and the police after them. We've got to get word to the police right away."

"But how?" asked Denny.

"That's a good question," said Uncle Frank. "You do as I say and you'll find out how. O.K.?"

"O.K.," Denny answered.

8) *The Capture*

"THERE'S ONE THING," said Uncle Frank. "We can't have Jessie staying here alone. No telling what those fellows up the Hollow might do. Might get that truck started and come down here and raise the devil. Somebody's got to stay here. Now Bert knows the lay of the land better—he'll stay and Denny and I'll get out of the Hollow in the jeep. Come on now, let's get going."

Bert knew better than to put up an argument when Uncle Frank laid down the law like that. "O.K.," he said, "I'll stay."

After the boys had changed to odds and ends of dry clothing and had eaten their dinner, Uncle Frank and Denny tossed a couple of picks and shovels into the jeep. Bert ran out of the house as the jeep was ready to start. "Take a good look at my place as you go by," he shouted. "I don't think the water got up to it, but you never know."

Uncle Frank called out that the house ought to be fine—he'd stop and see how it was anyway. He stepped on the gas and the jeep roared into the night.

For a few hundred feet the road looked perfectly normal. Then it dipped lower and closer to the Yankee Kill and the going became harder. Uncle Frank had to shift into four-wheel drive as the jeep bumped over places where the surface of the road had been washed away. "There's a bad place around the bend," Uncle Frank warned. "Hope we can make it." The headlights of the jeep picked out running water ahead. "Thought so," Uncle Frank said. He brought the jeep to a stop at the edge of the water. He and Denny piled out and sounded the water with their shovels. It seemed safe to go ahead—the water wasn't more than a foot deep.

They splashed through and began climbing a little as the road swung away from the Yankee Kill. They turned up a side road to the right. "We'll take a look at the old house and set Bert's mind at rest," said Uncle Frank. "It'll only take a minute." The jeep's headlights soon lit up the windows along the front of a weather-beaten house with a barn beside it.

"Looks fine," Uncle Frank announced. He began circling the barn to turn the jeep.

"Wait a minute," Denny said. "I hear something!"

Uncle Frank stopped and turned off the jeep's motor. From the house came the muffled barking of a dog. "Funny," said Uncle Frank, "there shouldn't be any dog in there." He switched off the jeep's headlights. "Look here," he whispered, "if there's a dog inside there may be a man—or two or three of them. No use both of us walking into trouble. I'll go up to the house and you stay here."

Denny sat still and peered at the house. When his eyes adjusted to the faint starlight he could make out the dark shape of the building against the darker mountain. He could see nothing of his uncle. Was he heading for the back door or the front door? Denny wished he'd told him. He felt left out of things with nothing to do but wait.

There was one thing he could do and that was to listen. The blackness all around seemed to make his ears keener and they picked up more and more little sounds —the rush of the Yankee Kill down the hill, the hoarse sound of a katydid far away, dozens of other insect sounds, the muffled voice of the dog that sounded a lot like Boot. There was the humming of the wind on the mountain. There were little rustlings, scrapings, and scratchings.

Then a welcome sound pierced the dark—the sound of an old tired door creaking open. Footsteps were heard on a wooden floor, and an overpowering shout, "Up with your hands! Don't move!"

Denny jumped out of the jeep.

That wasn't Uncle Frank's voice, yet it was a familiar voice. A moment of silence followed, then the beam of a flashlight shot out of the open front door of the house. There was an exclamation and a brief conversation. The barking of the dog went on but it sounded less whole-hearted, as if the dog was not quite sure he had some-

thing worth barking about. The human voices were cut
off roughly as the speakers went inside the house and the
door creaked shut after them. Something within the
house rattled and something bumped. The dog stopped
barking. Something came rushing toward Denny. From
out of the darkness Boot leaped into his lap, squirming
and squealing with joy, licking and sniffing in an effort
to express the wonder of meeting his master again.

"Come on, Denny." That was the voice of Uncle
Frank framed in the faint rectangle of light made by the
open door of the house. Denny felt his way up the path.
Boot jumped and circled around him as if all that was
going on was merely a glorious game. Inside the house a
dim kerosene lamp was trying hard to light the old-fashioned parlor. It glimmered on the old parlor organ, on
the roses scattered on the wallpaper, on the faces of
Uncle Frank and Dr. Bird, the bearded man.

The doctor gave Denny a smile and a vigorous hand-
shake. "I can imagine how surprised you must be to see
me and Boot," he said. "Well, I met your dog along the
road miles from Meech Hollow. He was with a bunch
of other dogs—probably they were running a deer, but
I don't know. I took Boot in my car, expecting to return
him to you after I'd taken a look over here."

"Boot doesn't run deer," Denny protested.

"You may be right," the doctor agreed. "Anyway, as
I came up Yankee Hollow the road vanished. Tons of
clay and gravel had been loosened by the rains and had

slid across the road. I was stuck. At the same time the Yankee Kill was rising fast. I had to get out of there or be marooned. Then I remembered that this place wasn't far away. So I came here. And I found I'd just missed meeting several other people."

"You missed what?" Uncle Frank asked.

"I'll show you," Dr. Bird answered. He carefully picked up the lamp from the table and led the way down a narrow hall to the kitchen at the back of the little house. He pointed to the long kitchen table. "All that stuff on the table was there when I got here—those packages of sandwiches and that thermos of hot coffee. So was that note." Dr. Bird pointed to a strip of brown wrapping paper beside the thermos.

" 'Gone up the road after the rest of the faces. Back soon.' " Denny read aloud. The faces . . . on reading these words Denny felt a tingle of excitement running through him. Were these the faces Bert had seen in the hideout?

Dr. Bird set the lamp on the table. "Somebody's been here a little while ago. And somebody intended to come back to meet someone else—from the amount of food here, half a dozen people must have been expected. I suspect some of those deer-jackers we've been hearing so much about were going to have a get-together here. Maybe the rain kept them from following through after they'd gotten those faces, whatever they may be."

"I know what they are," said Denny. "I saw the faces

up in the hideout." He explained about the masks and how Bert had been worried that he'd been seeing things that time he was alone in the hideout.

Uncle Frank said he was glad to have all that non-sense about devils in the Catskills cleared up: the deer-jackers had been frightening people with those masks. That was all there was to it. But how had the jackers gotten into the hideout to scare Bert? That was what he wanted to know.

"I think the answer is right here," said Dr. Bird. He picked up a small carton from the table and took out a gadget that looked a little like a camera. "It was here with the other stuff," he said. "Someone must have been planning to use the thing tonight." He tinkered with the gadget for a moment and then set it on the table. Something clicked softly. A pattern of light and shade appeared on the kitchen wall. "The masked men!" Denny exclaimed. "See—there's one of them on the bare wall beside the closet!"

"This thing is a slide projector with a timing device," said Dr. Bird. "It must have been in the hideout when Bert was there, and when it went on it threw the slide of those men with the masks on the wall for a moment. That would look eerie enough to scare anybody."

Uncle Frank said they ought to get out of there and let the police know. "This is their chance to get those two fellows. Now let's—"

Arh—Arh—Arh—Arh! Boot was barking furiously.

Lights flickered through the windows—they came from the headlights of two jeeps. Brakes squealed as the jeeps stopped almost on the doorstep.

"The jackers are here," Uncle Frank called. "Let's get out fast. The back door's the best way! We'll go up the mountain behind the house." Then he whispered, "Blow out that lamp."

The doctor leaned over the lamp and blew into the glass lamp chimney. Blackness seemed to fill the room as the light went out. Denny, Uncle Frank, and the doctor groped their way to the back door. Uncle Frank fumbled for the knob and at last threw the door wide open. It seemed to Denny in his eagerness that it had taken fifteen minutes to reach that door.

As the door swung open the look of the whole world seemed to change from darkness to a blaze of light. Powerful lights were focused on the three people standing at the back door. "Hands up. Don't move," someone ordered.

Denny looked at his uncle and the doctor. The two men glanced at each other. Then their hands rose in the air. Denny raised his.

Someone stepped out of the surrounding darkness into the light and began feeling the pockets of Uncle Frank and the doctor for weapons. The doctor started to protest. "Quiet," said a stern voice, "you may talk all you want to later."

Denny saw then that the men who had taken them

prisoners were not deer-jackers—they were state police-men.

A familiar face moved into the circle of light. It was that of Jesse Ames. Ames glanced at Uncle Frank and shook his head. Then he vanished into the darkness. A wave of anger came over Denny. Was it possible that the police thought Uncle Frank was a deer-jacker? Had they been taken in by that old song, "Billy Meech he had a gun"? Denny could hear the melody tinkling through his head. He fought down an impulse to shout aloud that his uncle and Dr. Bird were innocent. The only thing he could do was to stand there in silence.

The back door of the house opened and out stepped Denny's cousin Bill. The police didn't bother Bill; in fact one of them began talking to him in what seemed a confidential way. Nothing that had happened these last few minutes made sense—Bill's presence least of all.

Suddenly Bill's voice rang out, "What's that over by the barn? Isn't that my dad's jeep? What's Dad doing here?" Bill stared at the three prisoners. An alarmed look came over his face. "Something's wrong here," he shouted. "These aren't the jackers. Why, that's my dad there." He ran to his father and seized his arm.

Jesse Ames came out of the dark. "It's my mistake," he called. "You can all put your hands down. Sorry."

"You sure did made a mistake," Bill said. "When I told you I'd heard the gang of deer-jackers was going to cut up some deer in the barn over there tonight, I expected you'd round up the jackers and not my friends."

"I guess I owe you an explanation," Ames said to the group around him. "I thought Bill's tip would give us a fine chance to get the jackers with deer in their possession—they have ten deer hanging up in the barn. Then we'd have a case that would hold up in court. So I got the state police in to help, but I gave the word to move in too soon. I don't know yet what you folks are doing here. But that can wait. We've got to act fast before the real jackers get here."

The police jeeps and Uncle Frank's were quickly hidden in the woods behind the barn. Bill and Frank were stationed in the parlor to guard the house. "That dog's a real problem," said Ames. "Denny, you and the doctor go upstairs with the dog and keep him quiet—if he should bark he might give the whole show away. Keep a good grip on him and hold his muzzle if he shows signs of wanting to bark."

Denny settled down on the floor with one arm around Boot. The doctor sat beside him. For a while the sounds of the men below getting set for their vigil drifted up, and Denny and the doctor felt free to talk in whispers. "I have good news for Bill, but I haven't had a chance to give it to him yet," the doctor said. "Bill's going to get that one-thousand-dollar reward for finding a tree of the Golden Esopus apple. He found a tree in an old clearing in back of Sawtooth Mountain—it had been taken there a long time ago from your Hollow. I guess your people called it the Fence apple. It was my company that made the offer, but maybe you didn't know that."

"I didn't," Denny admitted, "and I can't imagine why anybody would pay that much for an old-time apple tree that nobody grows anymore."

"My company does research aimed at developing new sources of drugs and foods from plants. We've been working on a possible way of getting a higher vitamin C content into apples—because apples are low in vitamin C. We eat citrus fruits to get it into our diets. I found that here in the Catskills old-timers talked about an apple called the Golden Esopus which used to be believed to cure colds and other ailments and I wondered if this variety had what I was after. But I couldn't find a single tree anywhere. Hence the ad your uncle and Bill saw. We've found that it does have vitamin C—lots of it."

The footsteps of someone moving cautiously down below brought the doctor to a stop. Jesse Ames's voice came up the stairs. "Quiet now—no talking from now on. We're all ready for the jackers."

Twenty minutes went by—twenty minutes of listening to the sounds of insects, the gnawing of a mouse under the floor, and the hooting of a distant owl. Then Denny felt Boot stiffening. He struggled to free himself. A faint growl started to emerge from his mouth. Denny held the dog's struggling body while the doctor kept his hands firmly on Boot's muzzle. Soon a faint rumbling penetrated the house. A vehicle of some kind was traveling up the Hollow. As it came closer Boot's struggles increased, but he made no sound beyond a low stifled whine. The window of the little room glowed—the vehicle was approaching. "Quiet, Boot," Denny whispered, and Boot obeyed.

From the direction of the barn a mixture of little noises came. Doors were opened, a second vehicle arrived and stopped, low voices and cautious footsteps sounded. Boot struggled furiously and managed a fair-sized growl. At that moment—almost as if Boot had given the signal—all Yankee Hollow seemed to explode into a tumult of bangs and shouts. "Run!" someone shouted. A door banged harshly. People scuffled and cursed. "Watch that door, you dope!" someone shouted.

A loud voice was raised directly under the window beside which Denny and the doctor were crouching. Denny recognized the voice—it belonged to the man called Megoney. "I tell you he left the place right after those boys did," Megoney was protesting. "I waited awhile and then I got the motor going and came down here. I don't know where he is or what his real name is. I only met him the other day and he said his name was Ed James." It was plain enough that Ed James, who seemed to have been the leader of the jackers, had gotten away.

Denny and the doctor had promised to stay where they were and hang on to Boot until they were told to come downstairs, but it was hard for the two to keep from running down to see what was going on. They watched from the window as several vehicles left and the racket subsided to the accompaniment of a variety of growls and whines from Boot. At last Jesse Ames's voice came to the rescue of the two dog-watchers and Boot. "It's O.K. now—if you want to come down."

Down the stairs they rushed with Boot in the lead, barking valiantly. Jesse Ames and a state trooper were sitting beside the kitchen table. "Sit down, sit down," said Ames, pulling up two chairs. "Well, we got six of them. Only the one they call Ed James got away. Now, Denny, tell us what you know about this mess, what happened up at the place you call the hideout, and what these two fellows, Ed James and Megoney, said when they came to your house in the Hollow."

"Well," Denny began slowly.

"Take your time. Tell it any way you want to," Jesse Ames said.

The words began to pour out and Denny talked for ten minutes without a pause. There was only one thing he couldn't bring himself to tell—that was the way one of Ed James's ears hadn't colored like the other when he flushed. That seemed to be too crazy to be worth mentioning.

"That's all, then?" the trooper said. "There's nothing else you remember?"

Denny hesitated. "Well, there was one thing—"

"Yes, go ahead," the trooper urged. He listened attentively while Denny told of the odd behavior of James's ears.

"Thanks," he said. He smiled at Denny.

Up to that moment the day had been crammed with tension and excitement. But the trooper's smile seemed to mark the end of that. It seemed to say that now everything was getting back to normal and that the grown-up people were taking good care of things. The tiredness that had been building up inside Denny for hours hit him all at once. He wanted to go to sleep right where he was.

Everything that happened after that stuck in Denny's memory as a kind of sleepy blur. There was a lot of riding with Boot beside him in Uncle Frank's jeep, there was the jeep yanking Dr. Bird's car back on the road, there was the slow splashy trip down the Hollow, from which the flood was receding. And then there was Bert getting aboard.

At some point that state trooper was smiling at Denny again and saying that thanks to his description of James he was sure he'd be picked up any moment. James was really one-eared Jim Carey—a well-known gangster. One of his ears had been shot off in a fight and been replaced by an artificial one which wouldn't flush. He said Denny and Bert and Boot had done a lot to help round up the jackers, but both the boys were so tired they didn't even feel proud of themselves until later. As his jeep climbed up the Meech Hollow road, Uncle

Frank said wasn't it funny about those masks—they were copies of the ones farmers in the Catskills had used in what was called the Anti-Rent War a hundred years ago and more. There was still one up in the attic. He'd get it out and show it to the boys someday. His grandfather had worn it.

Everybody seemed to be talking at once at the Meech house that night: Dad and Mom, Uncle Frank and Dr. Bird. After Denny and Bert got in bed the voices kept on floating upstairs, but after a while they seemed to all melt together. And then Denny heard them tuning in Joe Woolsome's newscast. And he heard Joe saying that somebody named Denny Meech had gotten an A for a paper on the nomadic deer-jackers of the Catskills who wandered from hollow to hollow shooting deer at night. They had witch doctors who wore horrible masks and cured them when they fell and banged their legs. "Here's a bulletin," said Joe Woolsome. "One-eared Jim Carey, believed to be the head of the big deer-jacking operation in the Catskills, has just been arrested in the woods of Yankee Hollow. Now folks can sleep well in the Catskills again."

And at that Denny woke up for a moment, smiled to himself, and went back to sleep.